PEN

MORE TELEVI
OF M

Mr Majeika is a very special teacher, although only Thomas and Melanie know just *how* special. He is a wizard from Walpurgis and has been sent to Britland to teach Class Three at St Barty's School. He's not supposed to do anything magical, but sometimes he just can't help it . . . Magic and mayhem abound in these hilarious adventures, featuring the lovable and irrepressible Mr Majeika.

Humphrey Carpenter is the author of three Mr Majeika books which inspired the television series, *MR MAJEIKA, MR MAJEIKA AND THE MUSIC TEACHER* and *MR MAJEIKA AND THE HAUNTED HOTEL*, all published in Puffin. He has also written many books for adults and is co-author with his wife, Mari Prichard, of *THE OXFORD COMPANION TO CHILDREN'S LITERATURE*. He lives in Oxford and has two children.

Other books by Humphrey Carpenter

HUMPHREY CARPENTER

MORE TELEVISION
ADVENTURES
—— OF ——
MR MAJEIKA

Based on scripts by Jenny McDade
for the TVS production 'Mr Majeika'

PUFFIN BOOKS

PUFFIN BOOKS

Published by the Penguin Group
27 Wrights Lane, London W8 5TZ, England
Viking Penguin Inc., 40 West 23rd Street, New York, New York 10010, USA
Penguin Books Australia Ltd, Ringwood, Victoria, Australia
Penguin Books Canada Ltd, 2801 John Street, Markham, Ontario, Canada L3R 1B4
Penguin Books (NZ) Ltd, 182–190 Wairau Road, Auckland 10, New Zealand

Penguin Books Ltd, Registered Offices: Harmondsworth, Middlesex, England

First published by Puffin Books 1989
3 5 7 9 10 8 6 4 2
This text, based on scripts by Jenny McDade,
copyright © Humphrey Carpenter, 1989
All rights reserved

Filmset in Palatino
by Centracet, Cambridge

Made and printed in Great Britain by
Cox & Wyman Ltd, Reading

Dedicated
to Anna and Danny Forman
– and to Nigel Pickard and
Michael Kerrigan
who provided so many of the ideas!

CONTENTS

1

NANNY'S LITTLE
DARLING

Up in the sky, in the land of Walpurgis, where the wizards come from, the Worshipful Wizard was examining an enormous piece of paper. It was a graph, with a long wiggly line on it. At the head of it were the words:

Name: Majeika
Occupation: Teacher
Progress So Far

The wiggly line showed how well, or how badly, Mr Majeika was doing as a teacher down below in Britland.

The line started by going up. Mr Majeika had done very well at first. Then it went down. Down and down and down.

Mr Majeika had been sent down from Walpurgis, to be a teacher in Britland, because he was such a failure as a wizard. In fact he had failed his Sorcery Exams no less than seventeen times. And it was a rule that Failed Wizards, Third Class Removed, had to become teachers.

The place to which Mr Majeika had been sent was called Much Barty; a sleepy Britland village where nothing ever happened. At least, nothing ever happened there until Mr Majeika arrived. Then all of a sudden things started to happen very fast. Very surprising and peculiar things. Magic, in fact.

Mr Majeika wasn't supposed to do magic. Failed Wizards, Third Class Removed, who had been sent down to Britland to teach, were supposed to behave like ordinary Britland people, and do nothing Walpurgian. No changing of people into animals. No making things fly about in the air, no magical mending of things that had got broken, nothing out of the ordinary. But from the start, Mr Majeika kept forgetting this.

The first thing he had done, quite by accident, was to change Hamish Bigmore into a frog. Hamish Bigmore was the class nuisance in Class Three at St Barty's School. He was always showing off, and telling everyone how rich his parents were, and bullying people, and making a dreadful nuisance of himself, and suddenly Mr Majeika lost his temper on his first day at St Barty's School and turned Hamish Bigmore into a frog.

That caused a lot of trouble, particularly as Mr Majeika had forgotten the spell to turn Hamish back again. And later on there had been the School Fête, at which popcorn and ice-cream had rained down from the sky, and Hamish Bigmore had been smothered in a mountain of candy floss; and this was all because Mr Majeika had forgotten that he wasn't supposed to do anything Walpurgian, and kept flicking the tuft of his hair which meant that magic was about to happen. And later there had been some very peculiar goings on when a witch named Wilhelmina Worlock turned up, and there was a magic tree-house that built itself in the woods on a school trip, and other exciting happenings, all of which delighted Thomas Grey and Melanie Brace-Girdle.

Thomas and Melanie were special friends with Mr Majeika, and they were the only children in Class Three who knew that he was really a wizard. Hamish Bigmore and the rest of the class just thought he was a very peculiar-looking teacher to whom strange things happened. No one was supposed to know about him being a wizard, but Thomas and Melanie had spotted his secret almost as soon as he arrived at St Barty's School, and sometimes they had to help Mr Majeika get out of trouble by finding the right spell for him in his Spell Book.

The person with whom Mr Majeika was usually in trouble was the Worshipful Wizard. When Mr Majeika was sent down from Walpurgis to Britland, he found that he could still hear the Worshipful Wizard's voice in his ear, even though the Worshipful Wizard was miles and miles away, up there in Walpurgis. And the voice kept ticking him off and warning him, if he happened to flick his tuft and do anything Walpurgian.

Now Mr Majeika was about to start his second term at St Barty's School, and the Worshipful Wizard was going to make sure that he behaved much better than last term. He wanted the graph to show a real upward curve, to demonstrate some *real* progress. Because if Mr Majeika could really manage to be a good teacher and not do magic when he wasn't supposed to, he would be allowed to come back to Walpurgis and sit for his Sorcery Exams again.

'*Good morning, Majeika,*' said the voice of the Worshipful Wizard in Mr Majeika's ear. '*Your second term as a school teacher.*'

Mr Majeika was at his windmill home, just getting out the big black Walpurgian tricycle on which he rode to school every day. 'Oh, yes, sir,' he said to the Worshipful Wizard. 'Can't wait, sir.' Then he thought about Hamish Bigmore, and having to teach him – or try to teach him – for another term. 'Well, sir, I *almost* can't wait. Perhaps they wouldn't mind if I turned up a day or two late . . .?'

'*Nonsense, Majeika,*' said the Worshipful Wizard. '*No shirking. On your trike!*'

'Yes, sir,' said Mr Majeika sadly, pedalling off down the lane.

On the way to school, he passed Miss Lammastide, one of the village ladies, who was carrying a tray of fresh farm eggs back to her home, Wortle-berry Cottage. The eggs looked so inviting that Mr Majeika couldn't resist a little joke. He flicked his tuft, and there was a cracking and cheeping noise. Out of one of the eggs, a chick had hatched.

Miss Lammastide gave a little scream and dropped the eggs. '*Majeika!*' said the voice of the Worshipful Wizard, crossly, in Mr Majeika's ear. '*Nothing Walpurgian!*'

'Sorry, sir,' said Mr Majeika meekly. 'Slip of the tuft, sir.'

Up in Walpurgis, the Worshipful Wizard sighed and lengthened the line of the graph so that it curved even further downwards.

Further down the road, Mr Majeika triked past the Home for Distressed Teachers. 'Yoo-hoo!' called a voice. 'Yoo-hoo, Mr Majeika!' An elderly lady was leaning out of a window, waving to him.

This was Miss Flavia Jelley, who had taught Class Three before Mr Majeika came to St Barty's School. Miss Jelley was a very nervous sort of person – in fact when anything went wrong she shook just like a jelly – and after a few terms of trying to teach Hamish Bigmore, she had become a complete wreck. Mr Potter, the headmaster of St Barty's, had put her in the Home for Distressed Teachers, where she lived quite happily – provided that she didn't see Hamish Bigmore. If she hap-pened to catch so much as a glimpse of him being driven past the Home in his family's white Rolls-

13

Royce, she would scream and turn quite pale, and have to go to bed for several days.

'Good morning, Miss Jelley,' called out Mr Majeika rather gloomily. It was all right for her. *She* hadn't got to teach Hamish Bigmore any more. Mr Majeika wished someone would put *him* in a Home for Distressed Teachers.

Talking of Hamish, no sooner had Mr Majeika pedalled past the Home for Distressed Teachers than he could hear the horrible multi-toned horn of the Bigmores' white Rolls. As usual, the car nearly knocked him off his trike as it shot past, and as usual, Hamish was leaning out of the window pulling rude faces at him. For the umpteenth time, Mr Majeika wished that he'd never turned Hamish back from a frog into a boy. He'd have been in trouble with Walpurgis, but surely it would have been worth it . . .

But then something curious happened. The white Rolls had reached the crossroads just outside Much Barty, where you turned left to get into the village and to reach the school. But the Rolls had turned right!

Mr Majeika had no idea where the right-hand turning led to. He'd never looked closely at the signpost. As he pedalled up to it now, he read the sign. 'To Aerodrome,' it said.

Mr Majeika wondered what an Aerodrome was. Maybe an animal, or something you could eat?

'Come along, children,' called a bossy voice. Councillor Mrs Bunty Brace-Girdle, Melanie's mum, the

14

bossiest person in Much Barty, was acting as lollipop lady just outside St Barty's School, hustling the children across the road. Mr Majeika zoomed past her on his trike, gaily ringing his bell. 'Morning, Mrs Brace-Girdle,' he called, waving cheerily.

Mrs Brace-Girdle scowled. 'That little man,' she muttered. She didn't care in the least for Mr Majeika, in his peculiar clothes, with his big owl-like face and his hair like a mop. Strange things happened in Much Barty when he was around, and though Mrs Brace-Girdle had no idea he was a wizard, she was perfectly certain that there was something peculiar about him. She had much preferred that quiet Miss Jelley, even if the poor woman had always been quivering with nerves.

Quivering with nerves was what Mr Dudley Potter was doing right now. As headmaster, it was his job to make sure that everything ran smoothly at St Barty's School, but somehow it never did. How quickly the holidays had passed, and how quickly the start of the new term had arrived! He had read stories in which little boys had hated the idea of going back to school at the beginning of term. Well, how did they think the headmaster felt? He wished he could give it all up and stay at home doing crochet-work; he had made himself a very nice pair of bed-socks during the holidays. Now he wanted the time to make a night-cap with a woolly bobble. But with term beginning, there wouldn't be a chance.

'Hello, children!' he called, as he stood on the

school steps. 'Isn't it lovely to be back? Come along, everyone, time for morning assembly!'

He turned and went into the school hall, thinking sadly about the woolly night-cap that would never get made now. Then he remembered something which suddenly cheered him up. In fact, it cheered him up a great deal . . .

Mr Majeika squeezed his way into the hall just as the hymn was finishing. He was rather late because he had tried to make his trike park itself magically, and instead it had sped out into the road and chased a flock of sheep that Farmer Gurney was taking up to a field. It had taken Mr Majeika some minutes to get it back again, with a good deal of flicking of his tuft – to the accompaniment of disapproving noises from the Worshipful Wizard.

Mr Potter looked up from his hymn book and was very relieved to see that Mr Majeika had arrived. Odd things were always happening when Majeika was around, but somehow Majeika knew how to cope with Hamish Bigmore, which was more than Mr Potter did. Hamish Bigmore! Mr Potter suddenly remembered the good news and smiled to himself.

'Hello, Mr Majeika,' whispered Thomas, who was standing at the back of the hall next to Melanie. 'Nice to be back, isn't it, sir?'

Mr Majeika nodded and smiled at Thomas and Melanie. At the end of last term they had been terribly sad because they thought he was going back to Walpurgis to be a wizard again. But at the last minute Mr Majeika had got into trouble with Wizard Marks, the Walpurgian Examiner, and his Exit Visa from Britland had been cancelled. Thomas and Melanie had been delighted.

The hymn finished, and Mr Potter cleared his throat to make the announcements. 'Boys and girls, I'm afraid that I have some rather happy – I mean, sad – news to tell you. A unique and irreplaceable member of our school community is leaving us – departing for distant shores, whence he will never return. We must say farewell to a familiar figure at St Barty's.'

Mr Potter was trying to look sad, but really, the news was so good that a broad smile broke out on his face. He smiled straight at Mr Majeika. And though Mr Majeika hadn't the faintest idea what Mr Potter was smiling about, he smiled back.

Thomas and Melanie looked at each other, horrified. 'It isn't *you* that's going, is it?' Melanie whispered anxiously to Mr Majeika. Mr Majeika shook his head.

'So who is Mr Potter talking about?' whispered Thomas.

Mr Potter cleared his throat again. 'At this moment,' he announced, 'a charabanc, or what in common parlance is called a coach, is waiting to take us all to the Aerodrome, to say a fond farewell to this familiar figure. Come, children, I shall lead the way.' And he strode from the hall, with everyone following behind.

'Familiar figure?' said Melanie. 'Who can he mean?'

'I'll tell you one thing,' said Thomas. 'I haven't seen Hamish Bigmore this morning.'

'Hamish Bigmore!' muttered Mr Majeika, remembering that the white Rolls-Royce had turned down the road signposted 'To Aerodrome.' And that was where Mr Potter was taking everyone now. Well, at least he'd find out what an Aerodrome was.

In the coach, Mr Majeika sat next to Mr Potter. 'It, er, isn't Hamish Bigmore that's leaving, Mr Potter, is it?' he asked nervously, not daring to hope that it was true.

Mr Potter turned a smiling face to him. 'Yes, Majeika, isn't it wonderful? I mean, er, terribly sad? Hamish Bigmore is leaving us at last.'

Thomas was sitting in the seat just behind, and he heard the amazing news. 'Hey, listen everyone!' he shouted out. 'Hamish Bigmore is leaving us! Hamish is going for ever and ever and ever!'

The glad tidings spread throughout the bus and a great cheer went up from everyone. 'Hamish is going! Hamish is going! Hamish is going! HOORAY!!!

Much Barty Aerodrome was not a very big airport, certainly not as big as Heathrow or Gatwick. In fact, it wasn't really an airport at all. During the Second World War two or three very small aeroplanes had been stationed there, and when peace came a small flying club operated there for a while. There was still a control tower, where an ex-RAF pilot with a big moustache sat all day, hoping against hope that Concorde might come in to land there. But for most of the time there were no planes at all, just Farmer Gurney's sheep, who nibbled the grass on the edges of what had once been the runway.

Of late, though, one aircraft had been using the place: an antique Tiger Moth, left over from the Second World War, which Ronnie Bigmore flew for a hobby – and which he kept in readiness just in case, for one reason or another, he had to get out of Britain rather fast. Ronnie Bigmore had various 'business associates' who were known to the police. Indeed the police had been taking an interest in Ronnie himself; and a few days ago, Ronnie had decided that their interest was increasing to the point where he and the family might as well pack their bags and leave these shores, at least for the present.

So this morning the Tiger Moth was out on the grass, and Ronnie and Pam were unloading suitcases from the white Rolls, while Hamish sat in the back of the car chewing bubble gum.

'Good morning, everyone!' called a voice from the loudspeaker. It was the ex-RAF pilot speaking from the control tower. 'This is Barty Air Traffic Control welcoming you all to Barty Aerodrome, and announcing the departure of Bigmore Airways flight Big One, leaving for . . .' There was a rustling of paper as the ex-RAF pilot consulted an old map.

'Marbella, John,' said Ronnie Bigmore.

19

'. . . leaving for Marbella, John,' continued the loudspeaker. 'Please have your passports and boarding cards ready. Thank you. Have a nice day.'

At this moment the coach drove through the gate and into the Aerodrome. There was the sound of cheering. Everyone was still scarcely able to believe the good news. 'Hamish is going! Hooray, hooray, hooray!'

'Oh, isn't that nice, Hamish?' said Pam Bigmore, patting her son's head. 'All your little friends are so sorry to see you go that they've come to see you off, Hamish. Wave, Hamish.'

Hamish didn't wave. He blew out bubble gum so that it popped in Pam's face.

Mr Potter made a speech of farewell. He dabbed at his eyes with his handkerchief, trying to look sad. 'It only remains,' he said, 'for us to wish Hamish every happiness in his new life in a foreign land. I'm sure he will always remember Much Barty, and we in turn will never, *never* forget Hamish. Will we, Mr Majeika?'

Mr Majeika shook his head. 'Never, sir,' he said sincerely. 'How could we ever forget him?'

'Now, everyone,' called Mr Potter, 'three cheers for Hamish!'

There were wild cheers and renewed cries of 'Hamish is going! Hooray!'

Standing by the aeroplane, Pam Bigmore waved back. She couldn't quite hear what they were shouting. It sounded like 'Hamish is going, hooray!', but that couldn't be right; they all loved her little boy so. 'Bye, darlings,' she called out. 'Bye!'

'Get in,' muttered Ronnie, chucking the last suitcases into the back of the Tiger Moth. Hamish, scowling, clambered in on top of them. He could hear perfectly well what his schoolfellows were shouting. So they were delighted he was going, were they? One day he'd come back from Marbella and show them. He'd teach them to shout hooray!

Mr Majeika, waving goodbye alongside Thomas and Melanie, stared in puzzlement at the peculiar thing into which Pam, Ronnie and Hamish were climbing. He'd never seen anything like it in his life.

'What do you call that thing, Thomas?' he asked.

'A Tiger Moth,' answered Thomas, who knew quite a lot about old planes.

'It doesn't look like a tiger or a moth to me,' said Mr Majeika, shaking his head.

'Barty Control to Big One,' called the loud-speaker. 'You're cleared for take-off, Big One!'

'Outcha get and start it,' muttered Ronnie to Pam, and she clambered out of the cockpit and gave the propeller a twist, so that the engine spluttered into life.

Mr Majeika jumped with fright. 'Goodness!' he said. 'It certainly sounds like a tiger. And can it fly like a moth?'

'I hope so,' said Melanie. 'I certainly hope so.'

Pam clambered in, and the plane began to taxi

slowly across to the runway. 'Here we go,' muttered Ronnie. 'Hold on to your hats.' He opened the throttle, pulled back the joystick, and with a great deal of coughing and spluttering the old plane shot down the runway and began to lift into the sky.

A great cheer arose from Class Three and the other children – followed by a groan. The plane was dropping down to the ground again.

'Oh, no!' sighed Mr Potter. 'They're coming back! Have they changed their minds? I can't bear it!' And he hid his head in his hands.

Inside the cockpit, Ronnie was struggling with the controls. 'It's no use,' he muttered. 'We're too weighed down. Too much luggage.' Certainly with all Pam's suitcases and bundles of fashion magazines, the plane was far too heavy to take off.

'Out!' snorted Ronnie, reaching behind him and throwing out the first things he could find. 'Out, every bit of it!'

The baggage began to tumble out on to the aerodrome below. Farmer Gurney, who had just arrived with a lorry-load of sheep from another field, scowled up at the sky. 'Danged airyplanes!' he grumbled, as a pile of magazines and a make-up box just missed one of his best ewes.

'No, Ronnie!' shrieked Pam. 'Not my designer beachwear, Ronnie!'

'Out!' grunted Ronnie, throwing more stuff over the edge of the cockpit.

'Ronnie, not my copies of *Gracious Living for Folks with Loadsa Money*! Oh, Ronnie!'

'It's all gotta go,' said Ronnie. 'All of it. Every bit.' And now indeed the plane was lifting properly. It rose into the blue, soared over Much Barty church spire, and vanished over the horizon.

Mr Potter wiped his brow with relief. 'My, that was a narrow thing,' he said to Mr Majeika. 'But now we can say with certainty that we'll never see Hamish Bigmore again.'

'What's the point of going without our luggage, Ronnie?' sniffed Pam.

'Shuddup,' said Ronnie, as the plane reached the coast and began to cross the English Channel.

Pam sniffed again. 'Still, Ronnie, I'll say one thing. Hamish is being a really good boy, isn't he, Ronnie? He's so nice and quiet in the back there. So quiet that it's almost as if he wasn't there. Aren't you a good little boy, Hamish?' She turned round and smiled at the back seat. 'Hamish . . .? Oh, my goodness, Ronnie, he *isn't* there.'

The sheep were making quite a fuss in the back of their lorry. Something big and heavy had landed among them and had quite disturbed them. They baaed and baaed.

'Shut up, you danged old things,' grumbled Farmer Gurney. 'Out you comes.' He hooked each sheep with his crook and made it jump out of the lorry. Then he stopped and stared. 'Eee oop,' he said. '*You* bain't no sheep.'

Hamish Bigmore glared back at him.

* * *

23

'Well, well, Majeika,' beamed Mr Potter. 'It's quite over, quite, quite over, all that terrible nightmare of having to cope with Hamish Bigmore. And now the new life can begin. Life After Hamish, eh, Mr Majeika?'

Mr Majeika was staring at Farmer Gurney, who was advancing across the aerodrome with his crook around the neck of an all too familiar figure. 'This one of yourn?' he called to Mr Potter. 'Dratted kid, falling out of the sky and froightenin' moi sheep.'

'Oh dear,' said Mr Majeika. 'I don't know how to tell you this, Mr Potter, but I'm afraid that Life After Hamish can't begin quite yet.'

'It's no good,' said Melanie sadly, shaking her head. 'They'll never hear him.'

Mr Potter was standing in the middle of the runway, calling out to the sky: 'Come back! Come back! Mr and Mrs Bigmore! You've left Hamish behind! Come back!'

Thomas went up to the control tower. 'Can't you call them up on the radio?' he asked the ex-RAF pilot. 'Couldn't you tell them they've left Hamish behind, and ask them to come back and fetch him?'

The pilot shook his head. 'Afraid not, old chap. Barty Air Traffic Control doesn't actually have a radio. Anyway, do you think they'd really want him?' He gestured to the runway, where Hamish was managing to terrify Farmer Gurney's sheep by rushing at them with blood-curdling yells, pulling the most frightful faces at them.

Thomas shook his head. 'Maybe not,' he said gloomily.

That evening, Mr Potter called an urgent meeting of the Friends of St Barty's School. Most of the parents, sensing that something unpleasant might be asked of them, did not turn up. Around Mr Potter's study table, sipping tea from his olde worlde china cups, sat only a few of the local ladies, including Councillor Mrs Brace-Girdle and her friend Miss Lammastide.

'You understand the problem, ladies,' said Mr Potter gloomily. 'A homeless pupil who needs to be housed. And so it is with not a little urgency that I ask, which of you lucky people would like to have Hamish Bigmore as a guest in your home, until his parents come back for him?'

There was a long silence. Mr Potter looked around the table without much hope. 'Miss Lammastide?' he said.

Miss Lammastide shook her head. 'I'm afraid not, Mr Potter. You see, my spare room houses my library.'

'Library, Miss Lammastide?'

'My library of Style Easy knitting patterns, Mr Potter.'

'Ah, yes,' said Mr Potter. 'Mrs Brace-Girdle, you have a spare room, have you not?'

'Mr Brace-Girdle sleeps in my spare room, Mr Potter,' answered Mrs Brace-Girdle.

'Quite so.' Mr Potter looked around the room again. 'No one else?'

The door from Mr Potter's kitchen opened, and Hamish Bigmore walked in, munching Mr Potter's supper, which he had stolen from the fridge. 'Looks like I'll be staying with you, then, Mr Potter!' he said cheerfully. 'Doesn't it?'

Mr Potter turned rather white. 'Yes, Hamish,' he said, gritting his teeth. 'And won't that be lovely?'

After the meeting had dispersed, Melanie and Thomas went to Mr Potter's study with Mr Majeika. 'We've got an idea, Mr Potter,' said Melanie. 'We think you should phone the Bigmores in Marbella.'

Mr Potter was looking very shaky. 'I don't think I feel up to phoning anyone, Melanie,' he said. 'I'm going to retire to bed and take some of my nerve pills. Could you phone, Majeika?'

'Yes, Mr Potter,' said Mr Majeika doubtfully, as the headmaster tottered up the stairs to his bedroom. 'Leave it to me, Mr Potter.' He looked vaguely around the study. 'Phone?' he said to Thomas and Melanie. 'What's a phone?' He picked a bunch of flowers out of a vase. 'Is it a kind of flower?'

Thomas shook his head. 'It's this thing on the desk, Mr Majeika,' he said, pointing at the telephone. 'You put it to your ear.'

Mr Majeika picked up the entire telephone and

put the flat bottom of it to his ear. 'Like this?' he asked.

'No,' said Melanie. 'Just this bit here.' She showed him how to use the receiver, and she dialled the operator.

'Can I help you?' said the operator's voice in Mr Majeika's ear.

Mr Majeika dropped the phone in horror. 'There's someone in there!' he cried. 'Britland magic!' He mopped his brow nervously.

Mr Potter appeared at the door of the study. 'I can't sleep for worry,' he explained. 'Are you through to Marbella yet, Majeika?'

Mr Majeika shook his head. 'Not yet, Mr Potter. I don't think it's going to be easy.'

'Never mind,' said Mr Potter. 'I have an idea.'

By now, Hamish Bigmore was making his presence in School Cottage thoroughly felt. He had taken Mr Potter's radio into the spare bedroom and was playing very, very loud music. The whole house was shaking.

In his study, Mr Potter was shaking too. But he was determined to do something about his idea. He had a plan which he was convinced would help him cope with Hamish.

He was writing out a card to put in the window of Much Barty Post Office. 'Nanny wanted,' he wrote. 'Urgently.' Then he crossed this out and put 'VERY urgently'. He thought for a moment, then added: 'Small salary offered to plucky applicant.' Then he crossed out 'plucky' and changed it to 'lucky'. He thought he might as well make the job sound attractive.

Upstairs, Hamish's music blared on, as Hamish lay in bed, eating some chocolates he had found in Mr Potter's sitting room, and smearing his sheets with the gooey ones he didn't like.

The next afternoon, Mr Majeika was taking Class Three for a game of football on the school playing-field. 'Play nicely, Hamish,' he pleaded, for Hamish Bigmore was behaving worse than ever. He had twice booted the ball on to the roof of a shed, making it almost impossible to get it down, and whenever Thomas turned his back, Hamish came up and kicked him on the ankles. Clearly he was going to be even more of a nuisance than usual, now that Pam and Ronnie weren't around to keep some sort of eye on him.

Mr Majeika blew his whistle for half-time, and sat down at the edge of the field. 'It's no good, is it?' said Thomas. 'There's nothing we can do, Mr Majeika, to get Hamish's parents to come back and fetch him?'

Mr Majeika shook his head mournfully. 'I'm afraid not, Thomas,' he sighed.

Just then there came a voice from the road. 'Yoo-hoo! Mr Majeika!'

Mr Majeika and Thomas turned round. A large pram was pushing itself down the road. On closer inspection, someone could be seen pushing it – an elderly lady rigged out in a nanny's uniform, with starched collar and a neat little cap.

'Crikey,' said Melanie, who had come up to have a look. 'Who is it? Mary Poppins?'

'Yoo-hoo!' called the nanny. 'Mr Majeika, yoo-hoo, it's me!'

Mr Majeika stared. 'Flavia!' he said. 'Flavia Jelley! What a surprise! How nice to see you, Miss Jelley. Better, I hope?'

'Much better, thank you,' smiled Miss Jelley, only shaking a very little bit as she spoke. 'So much better that I'm going to apply for a job.'

'A job, Miss Jelley?' said Mr Majeika. 'As a teacher?'

'Oh no,' said Miss Jelley. 'I wouldn't want to go anywhere near – ' and her voice dropped as she muttered the awful name, ' – *Hamish Bigmore*. No, I'm going to be a nanny instead. I'm answering an advertisement in the post office.'

'A nanny, Miss Jelley? What's a nanny?' said Mr Majeika.

'A nanny is someone, Mr Majeika, who looks after other people's little darlings. And I'm hoping to look after a little darling at School Cottage.'

'At School Cottage, Miss Jelley?' said Mr Majeika, who knew nothing about Mr Potter's advertisement.

'Yes, Mr Majeika. At School Cottage. Dear Dudley, Mr Potter, has been advertising for a nanny to look after a little darling. And I just can't wait to see the sweet little creature!'

Miss Jelley rang Mr Potter's doorbell.

'Why, Flavia!' said Mr Potter as he opened the

door. 'What a lovely surprise. But why the, er, uniform?'

'Your advertisement, Dudley,' said Miss Jelley. 'I'm answering it. Don't worry, Dudley, Nanny Jelley will soon have everything all cosy and spick and span for the little darling. Now, do tell me, Dudley, is it a sweet little girl, or a sweet little boy?'

Mr Potter gulped. 'Well, Flavia, you'd better come and see.'

Hamish Bigmore was changing out of his football clothes. He had reduced Mr Potter's spare bedroom to ruins already. He turned on the radio full blast.

The door opened, and Mr Potter's head appeared round it. 'I've a surprise for you, Hamish,' he called out over the noise.

'Uh huh?' grunted Hamish without interest. 'Wot is it? Biggest box of chocs in the world or sumfink?'

Mr Potter opened the door fully. In the doorway stood Nanny Jelley.

'Your new nanny, Hamish,' said Mr Potter.

Nanny Jelley looked at him, opened her mouth and began to scream.

'Oh no,' muttered Hamish Bigmore. 'Not *her* again.'

Mr Majeika, Thomas and Melanie were on their way back to school when Miss Jelley passed them at top speed, pushing her pram and still scream-ing. 'She must have been introduced to her little darling,' remarked Thomas.

Mr Potter was running after her, desperately waving his arms. 'Flavia!' he was calling. 'Nanny Jelley! You can't leave us! You're our last hope!'

'We'd better do something, Mr Majeika,' said Melanie.

They ran after Miss Jelley, caught up with her, sat her in her own pram (which was just big enough to hold her like a wheelchair), and pushed her all the way back to School Cottage.

'There, there, Miss Jelley,' said Mr Majeika soothingly. 'Don't be so anxious. He's only a little boy.'

'He's not a little boy,' gasped Miss Jelley. 'He's a monster.' She began to sob. 'And I wanted Christopher Robin, Mr Majeika.'

'Christopher who?' asked Mr Majeika.

'But Christopher Robin doesn't live in Much Barty, Miss Jelley,' said Thomas. 'And Hamish Bigmore does.'

'Look at it this way, Miss Jelley,' said Melanie. 'He's just a poor little boy . . .'

'. . . who's been left behind by his parents,' said Thomas.

'And who fell out of an Iron Fly,' said Mr Majeika.

'An Iron Fly?' asked Miss Jelley in astonishment.

'He means an aeroplane,' said Melanie.

'Into the arms of his friends,' said Mr Majeika.

'But Hamish hasn't got any friends,' pointed out Miss Jelley.

'No, Miss Jelley,' agreed Melanie, with something of her mother's firm, bullying tone. 'But he's got a nanny who's agreed to look after him. So oughtn't nanny to get on with the job?'

Miss Jelley began to quiver all over, stuffing her handkerchief into her mouth to stop herself from screaming again.

Thomas sighed, and took Mr Majeika on one side. 'Can't you do *something*, Mr Majeika? For her, I mean?'

Mr Majeika scratched his head. 'Me, Thomas? What sort of thing?'

'Put a spell on her or something. Well, you are a wizard.'

'Ssh!' whispered Mr Majeika. 'No one's supposed to know. And anyway, only a Failed Wizard of the Third Class Removed.'

But there must be *something* magical you could do,' whispered Melanie, coming up to them. 'Let's go to the windmill and have a look in your Spell Book.'

If you had looked through the window of Mr Majeika's windmill a little later that evening, you would have seen a row of bubbling flasks and glass jars, with mysterious tubes and pipes connecting them, and steam of many colours rising out of it all. Mr Majeika was making a magical potion.

Thomas and Melanie had looked through the

Spell Book and found a spell headed: 'How To Give A Lady A Will Of Iron.'

'Has Walpurgis ever turned anyone into an Iron Lady before, Mr Majeika?' asked Melanie.

'Only once,' said Mr Majeika. 'I believe she was a grocer's daughter from Grantham. I wonder what happened to her.' He was looking carefully in the Spell Book. 'Oh no,' he frowned.

'What's the matter?' asked Melanie.

Mr Majeika pointed out some words in the spell to Thomas. 'Can only be successful,' read Thomas out loud, 'if administered at night-time under a Hickory Moon.'

'Is it a Hickory Moon tonight, Mr Majeika?' asked Melanie.

'I've no idea,' answered Mr Majeika sadly. 'And anyway, I'm certainly not allowed to go administering spells to anyone under any sort of moon. Walpurgis has absolutely forbidden it, Melanie.'

'This won't do,' said Melanie briskly, sounding just like her mother. 'For a start, let's find out about the moon.'

She switched on Mr Majeika's Walpurgian radio set. As it happened, just at that moment the Worshipful Wizard was finishing the day's programmes. *'And so,'* they heard his voice saying, *'on behalf of the Walpurgian World Service, broadcasting to all wizards in foreign parts, especially in Britland, it only remains for me to wish you all a delightful dance under tonight's Hickory Moon. And to all Failed and Unqualified Wizards, such as Wizard Majeika, down there in Much Barty, mind you behave yourselves and*

33

*spend a quiet night in your hammocks. Goodnight,
Majeika!'*

'Goodnight, sir,' muttered Mr Majeika guiltily,
switching off the radio and picking up the jar of
Iron Lady potion which he had mixed. Putting his
finger to his lips, he tiptoed to the door.

'Do you want us to come with you?' whispered
Thomas.

Mr Majeika shook his head. 'Better stay here,'
he whispered back. 'I don't want to get you both
in trouble. I shall be in a bad enough pickle myself
if the Worshipful Wizard finds out.'

It was a full Hickory Moon and the owls were
hooting. Mr Majeika triked as quietly as he could
up to School Cottage, hoping that the voice of the
Worshipful Wizard wouldn't suddenly speak in
his ears, asking him what he was up to out in the
moonlight. But evidently they were all asleep up
in Walpurgis.

Everyone at School Cottage was asleep too.
Hamish, stuffed with chocolates, was snoring in
Mr Potter's spare bed. Mr Potter himself was
tossing and turning restlessly, dreaming that he
was sending telegrams, carrier pigeons and smoke
signals to Marbella, demanding that the Bigmores
come back and take Hamish off his hands. Nanny
Jelley was asleep, but she was not in bed. She was
sleep-walking.

Up and down the kitchen she paced, clutching
her hot-water bottle and muttering to herself, 'I
can't stand it! I can't stand it! I can't stand it!'

Mr Majeika parked his trike and tiptoed up to the kitchen window. He watched poor Nanny Jelley as she strode up and down. And he saw that just inside the window, on the kitchen table, stood a mug of cocoa with the name 'Nanny' on it.

Very quietly, he opened the window, uncorked the Iron Lady potion, and began to pour some drops into the cocoa.

Back in the windmill, Thomas was turning over the pages of the Spell Book as he and Melanie waited for Mr Majeika to return.

'I've just remembered something,' said Thomas, yawning. 'In the instructions for the Iron Lady potion, it says: "Warning, do not exceed three drops." Do you think Mr Majeika knows that?'

'I hope so,' said Melanie.

'Because it says: "If this dose is exceeded, patient will turn into a Hectoring Harridan."'

'What's a Hectoring Harridan?' asked Melanie.

'I don't know, Mel,' said Thomas. 'But whatever it is, it doesn't sound very nice.'

At the kitchen window at School College, Mr Majeika was counting the drops of the Iron Lady potion as he poured them into the cocoa. 'Thirty-four, thirty-five, thirty-six . . . I think that should do it,' he whispered to himself. 'I think it said something about "Do not exceed thirty-six drops." Now, come on, Nanny Jelley,' he called softly. 'Nice drinkies, Nanny Jelley.'

Miss Jelley sleep-walked across the room, and picked up the mug.

'Nice drinkies,' cooed Mr Majeika again.

Miss Jelley swigged the lot.

Mr Potter's dreams had stopped at last and he had fallen into a deep slumber.

Suddenly he was rudely awoken. The light had been turned on and someone was briskly pulling the bedclothes off him. 'Out of your pit, Potter!' roared a powerful female voice.

Mr Potter blinked and stared. 'Good gracious!' he said. 'Flavia! Nanny Jelley! Are you all right?'

The Hectoring Harridan who had once been Nanny Jelley grasped Mr Potter's shoulders with a grip of steel. 'I said OUT OF BED!' she roared in the voice of a Regimental Sergeant-Major.

Hamish Bigmore was dreaming his usual dream of bullying the smallest children in the school and refreshing himself with a giant box of chocolates, when he too woke to find the light on and a figure, ramrod stiff, standing at the end of his bed and roaring at him.

'Out of bed, Bigmore!'

Hamish blinked and rubbed his eyes. 'Go away,' he said. 'It's the middle of the night.'

'At the DOUBLE, Bigmore!' roared the voice, and Hamish found himself catapulted out of bed on to the floor.

A few minutes later, if you had been standing by the kitchen window at School Cottage, you would have seen Mr Potter and Hamish, who had struggled into their clothes, being herded into the kitchen by Nanny Jelley as if they were Farmer Gurney's sheep.

'What time do you call this to be on parade, you lazy-bones?' roared the fearsome woman in the nanny's uniform who had once been a quivering wreck. 'Come on now, get those knees up, one two! One two!'

After half an hour of parade-ground drilling, they were ordered to clean their shoes.

'And what do I want to see in those shoes, Potter?' snapped Miss Jelley in her Iron Lady voice.

'Feet?' asked Mr Potter, quaking.

'No, I want them shining so much that I can see my face in them, don't I? Say "Yes, Nanny Jelley."'

'Yes, Nanny Jelley,' said Mr Potter meekly.

'And as for you, Bigmore,' roared the Iron Lady, 'I want to see your school uniform buttons buffed up so that they sparkle. Spit and polish, that's the thing, or you'll be on Defaulters' Parade doing square-bashing for two hours.'

'Huh,' muttered Hamish. 'You'll be lucky.'

Miss Jelley picked him up by the scruff of the neck. 'Say "Yes, Nanny Jelley!"' she ordered in her thundering voice.

'Yes, Nanny Jelley,' said Hamish.

Thomas and Melanie, yawning after their late night, were walking to school with some of their

37

friends, when they heard a powerful voice coming from the front door of School Cottage. 'Squad, by the left, qui—ck *march*! Left, right, left, right, come along, swing those arms. Left, right, left right.'

From the front door there emerged two marching figures, Mr Potter and Hamish Bigmore. Behind them, with a stick under her arm, marched Nanny Jelley.

'Left, right, left, right!' she roared.

Mr Potter blinked miserably at the children, but did not dare to say anything. Then Nanny Jelley saw Thomas and Melanie and the others. 'Come along, you shirkers. Who gave *you* a stand easy order? Into file, crocodile!'

Reluctantly, Thomas, Melanie and the rest of them got into line, and Nanny Jelley marched them into school.

'Look at Hamish Bigmore out with his Nanny!' laughed Thomas.

'Quiet at the back, there!' roared Nanny Jelley. It was obvious that it was not only Hamish Bigmore who was to be kept under control!

'I think that Mr Majeika must have given her more than three drops of that potion,' whispered Melanie. 'This could be tricky!'

By the end of the morning, Nanny Jelley had reduced the whole school to exhaustion. She had had all the children, Mr Potter and Mr Majeika out in the playground marching up and down under her orders. Now she had allowed them just ten minutes for lunch.

Thomas, Melanie and Mr Majeika decided to miss lunch and hurry to the windmill to see if they could find an antidote to the Iron Lady potion.

'Let's see,' said Mr Majeika, turning the pages. '"Women into Ninnies." No, that's no good. "Women into Nannies." Ah, that should do, it'll turn her into an ordinary nanny again, I suppose.'

'Have you read the spell properly?' asked Thomas. 'You never bother to read the small print, Mr Majeika. That's why you're still a Failed Wizard.'

'No time,' gasped Mr Majeika. 'We'll have to get back to school quickly, or Nanny Jelley will put us on Defaulters' Parade.'

'*That's not your spell book you've got there, is it, Majeika?*' said the voice of the Worshipful Wizard suddenly in Mr Majeika's ear.

'Oh, no, sir, good gracious no,' muttered Mr Majeika, hastily stuffing the Spell Book under his coat and beckoning to the two children. 'Come on, you two,' he whispered to them, 'before *he* finds out. I don't want to get into more trouble with Walpurgis.'

Nanny Jelley was blowing her whistle and ordering everyone on parade when they got back to school.

'Come on, you stragglers!' she shouted at Thomas, Melanie, and Mr Majeika. 'Form up!'

'*Now*,' said Mr Majeika, muttering the spell to himself and waggling his tuft of hair.

39

There was an explosion and a puff of smoke and Nanny Jelley was nowhere to be seen.

'Well,' said Melanie, 'something's happened. But where is she?'

From behind them there came a *baa*. 'What is it?' asked Thomas, turning round. 'One of Farmer Gurney's sheep?'

Melanie shook her head. 'No,' she said. 'It's a goat. You've changed her into a nanny all right, Mr Majeika. A nanny goat.'

Mr Potter bustled out of School Cottage and nearly ran into the goat. 'Mr Majeika! Mr Majeika!' he called. 'It's come at last! A missive with a Marbella postmark!'

He was holding out an airmail letter that the postman had just delivered. He ripped it open and read it out with glee: '"Dear Mr Potter, Arriving Barty Aerodrome three p.m. Please meet us with Hamish. Gratefully yours, the Bigmores." They're coming back, Mr Majeika! They're coming back to collect Hamish! Isn't that a relief?'

'Yes,' said Mr Majeika. 'It certainly is.'

'By the way,' said Mr Potter, 'what's that goat doing here?'

'Goat, Mr Potter?' said Mr Majeika, flicking his tuft. The goat vanished. 'What goat, sir?'

Mr Potter looked around him and scratched his head. 'Oh, er, no, there isn't one, is there? Well, let's be off to the Aerodrome. I'll order the chara-banc and this time we really will see him off.' He bustled away to telephone.

'Mr Majeika,' said Melanie, 'if the goat has vanished, where is Miss Jelley?'

Mr Majeika thought for a moment. 'I don't know, Melanie. I really don't know. What's the time? We ought to be off to the Aerodrome if the Iron Fly is coming back again.'

Thomas looked at the church clock. 'It's a quarter to three,' he said. 'And there's Miss Jelley.'

Melanie looked. 'Yes, what on earth is Miss Jelley doing on top of the church tower, Mr Majeika?'

Mr Majeika sighed. 'Oh dear,' he sighed. 'I really am still a Failed Wizard, aren't I? How on earth did I manage to magic her up there?'

Miss Jelley, who was clearly no Iron Lady any longer, was sprawled across the weathercock, and screaming and waving frantically from the very top of the church spire. 'Help! Help, Mr Majeika! Get me down!'

'Turn left by that lighthouse, Ronnie,' said Pam Bigmore, studying the map and looking out of the window of the Tiger Moth, 'and Much Barty is about a couple of miles further on. Oh, Ronnie, I can't wait to see my little Hamish again.'

'Huh,' grunted Ronnie.

The plane flew on towards Much Barty. Soon they were passing the church tower.

'That's funny, Ronnie,' said Pam. 'I could have sworn there was someone on the church spire. Someone in a sort of nurse's uniform, waving and shouting.'

'Huh,' said Ronnie.

'I know you think I'm talking rubbish, Ronnie, but really there was.'

'Huh,' said Ronnie.

They flew on for a few moments, and then Pam spoke again.

'Ronnie?'

'Huh.'

'D'you know there are two people sitting out there on the wing of the plane, Ronnie?'

'Huh! Don't be – '

'Yes, Ronnie, really there are. And one of them is tapping on the cockpit window, Ronnie. It's Mr Majeika, Ronnie. And the other one is the person in the nurse's clothes.'

'So sorry to bother you, Mrs Bigmore,' said Mr Majeika as Pam opened the plane window. 'My friend Miss Jelley here happened to be stuck on the church weathercock, so I just flew up – I mean, climbed up – to rescue her. And since she was too nervous to climb down, I took advantage of your plane as it was passing by. Thank you for the lift.'

'Huh?' said Ronnie Bigmore in astonishment, landing the plane at Much Barty Aerodrome.

Mr Potter, Class Three, and all the other children were lined up along the runway, cheering, as the plane came in to land. When it had taxied to a stop, Mr Majeika climbed out, carrying poor Miss Jelley, who by now had quite fainted away from fright.

When the cheering had stopped, Mr Potter led

Hamish to the front of the crowd. 'Here he is, Mr Bigmore,' he called out to Ronnie. 'Here is your dear son, all packed and ready to leave for Marbella, Mr Bigmore.'

'Mummy's little precious!' cried Pam, climbing out of the plane and embracing Hamish.

'Geddoff!' muttered Hamish, pushing her away.

'Well, Hamish,' said Mr Potter, 'wave goodbye to all your little friends for the last time.'

'Nah,' said Ronnie Bigmore from the cockpit of the plane. 'Nah, John. You got it all wrong.'

'Nah?' said Mr Potter vaguely.

'Nah. You ain't got the drift, see. We oughter written a letter t'explain, John, but the missus 'ere wanted to pop back and see the kid. Yer see, John, the point is that after thinking about it, me an' the missus would like Hamish to 'ave a proper good English education.'

'Ah,' said Mr Potter vaguely. 'Yes, I see.'

'Like wot we 'ad, John,' said Ronnie Bigmore.

'Ah,' said Mr Potter. 'An English education? Not . . . in Marbella?'

'Nah,' said Ronnie Bigmore. 'Not in Marbella, John. 'Ere, in Much Barty. We wants to leave 'im, to leave 'Amish, in your capable 'ands.'

'*Leave* him?' said Mr Potter, unbelievingly. '*Leave* . . . *Hamish*? You mean, Hamish is to – to *remain* here?'

'Wiv you,' said Ronnie Bigmore.

'Permanently?' gasped Mr Potter. 'All the time?'

'Yeah, John.'

Mr Potter, white faced, turned to Mr Majeika.

'Oh, isn't that good news, Mr Majeika?' he said in a strangled voice. 'Hamish is to stay with us. For ever.'

Miss Jelley, who had just come round from her fainting fit, fainted again.

'So you didn't lose your little friend after all, Majeika?' said the voice of the Worshipful Wizard, as Mr Majeika was back at the windmill that evening, trying to put up a Britland deckchair in his garden. He wanted to sit down and go to sleep and forget about the fact that he would have to teach Hamish Bigmore for ever and ever and ever.

'Unfortunately not, sir,' he answered.

'Still, I'm sure he'll be a joy to you in days to come.'

'If you say so, sir,' said Mr Majeika gloomily.

'Carry on, Majeika!'

Mr Majeika sat down heavily in the deckchair, which collapsed under his weight.

'Yes, sir,' he said sadly.

2

GENIE WITH THE LIGHT BROWN LAMP

It was a bright sunny morning and Mr Majeika was just off to school. He whistled for his trike, which rolled up to the steps of the windmill, ringing its bell in a friendly fashion.

'*Morning, Majeika,*' said the voice of the Worshipful Wizard. '*Off so bright and early?*'

'That's right, sir,' said Mr Majeika cheerfully. 'Time for school as usual.'

'*Really, Majeika? Do you know what date it is?*'

Mr Majeika thought for a moment. 'No, sir. I haven't the faintest idea.'

'*In the Walpurgian calendar, Majeika, it's the ninety-fifth of Hecate. Which in Britland would make it about the twenty-fifth of July.*'

'Oh, sir, is that so?'

'*Yes, Majeika.*'

'And what difference does that make, sir?' asked Mr Majeika, thoroughly puzzled.

'*You'll see, Majeika,*' chuckled the Worshipful Wizard. '*You'll see.*'

* * *

Mr Potter was padlocking the school gates and putting up a notice which said: 'School Closed. Will reopen on September 3rd.'

He sighed with happiness. Six whole weeks of holidays! Six whole weeks without all the worries of school life! Six whole weeks without . . . He remembered something he had to do before he left Much Barty for his seaside boarding-house. He got on his motor cycle and zoomed off up the road towards Councillor Mrs Brace-Girdle's house.

No sooner had he gone than Mr Majeika came into view, triking anxiously down the road. The Worshipful Wizard had got him worried. Did St Barty's School turn into a pumpkin on the twenty-fifth of July, or something awful like that? He couldn't wait to find out.

In a moment he *had* found out. The school gates were locked, secured with a big chain and there was a 'School Closed' notice.

Closed! He'd never heard of such a thing! It was his job to teach there, every weekday. Nobody had told him it was going to close. This was terrible! How was he supposed to fill the time till the school reopened? And when was September? For all he knew, it might be in a hundred years from now.

Desperately, he began to shake the gates. 'Mr Potter!' he called out miserably. 'Mr Potter! It's me, Mr Majeika! Please open up! I've got nowhere to go, nothing to do and I can't wait until September!'

Mr Potter was now half a mile away, at Mrs Brace-Girdle's cottage. Mrs Brace-Girdle was doing some

46

gardening when he arrived, snipping the dead heads rather fiercely off her roses. It was a hot day and she was getting bad-tempered. Thomas Grey's parents had gone abroad and left Thomas to stay with the Brace-Girdles, and Mrs Brace-Girdle resented having the extra mouth to feed. It wasn't as if she had time for a foreign holiday herself, with all her Committees. After all, *someone* had to keep Much Barty running smoothly.

'Ah, Bunty,' called out Mr Potter cheerfully, climbing off his motor cycle and pushing up his goggles.

Mrs Brace-Girdle smiled at him rather frostily. 'Off on *your* holidays as well, Mr Potter? Some of us don't have time for holidays, you know.'

Mr Potter was in too happy a mood to notice her grumpiness. 'Yes, yes, I'm off to Barty Bay as usual. I've booked in with Mrs Laburnum at Marine View, where I stay every year.'

'How nice for you,' said Mr Brace-Girdle frostily.

'Hot and cold running water in every room,' said Mr Potter happily. 'And she makes you sandwiches to take to the beach. One does get a little tired of the cold beef and semolina pudding *every* night, but at Mrs Laburnum's prices, one can't complain.'

'I'm sure one can't,' said Mrs Brace-Girdle impatiently. 'Melanie! Thomas!' she called. 'Do come and help me in the garden! I've got so much to do. And if there's nothing else you want, Mr Potter . . .'

'Well, Bunty,' said Mr Potter, 'there was just one

thing. I so need my holiday, you know – the doctor says that absolute peace and quiet is essential for my nerves – and I wonder if you wouldn't mind, while I'm away, taking care of . . .'

He lifted the lid of his motor-cycle sidecar, and a familiar, unwelcome face looked out.

'. . . Hamish Bigmore,' finished Mr Potter.

'Hamish Bigmore, Mr Potter?' said Mrs Brace-Girdle, dropping her shears and staring in disbelief.

'Hamish Bigmore?' chorused Thomas and Melanie, emerging from the house.

'Only for a fortnight,' cooed Mr Potter. 'I'm sure we can make some other arrangement after that.'

'It's quite out of the question,' said Mrs Brace-Girdle firmly. 'I've already got Thomas Grey staying, not to mention the school guinea-pig and a tank of school tadpoles.'

'I know it's a lot to ask, Bunty,' said Mr Potter, using all his powers of persuasion, 'but no one else has the strength of character to cope with Hamish.'

Bunty Brace-Girdle paused. This was rather flattering.

'There's no one else in the village I would ask,' went on Mr Potter, 'because no one else has the boundless good nature and the resourcefulness to cope. Naturally, Bunty, I turned to you. Who else is there?'

'Yes,' said Bunty Brace-Girdle thoughtfully. 'Who indeed? Well, if you put it like that . . .'

'Oh no!' said Thomas and Melanie.

'Couldn't someone else have him, Mr Potter?' asked Melanie.

'I did, of course,' said Mr Potter, 'think of Mr Majeika. But unfortunately he wasn't in when we called at the windmill, was he, Hamish?'

'No,' smirked Hamish.

'Well then,' said Mrs Brace-Girdle, 'only for a fortnight . . .'

Mr Majeika was standing miserably in the middle of Much Barty's main street, looking around him. The whole place was deserted.

'Where is everybody, sir?' he asked the Worshipful Wizard.

'Gone off on their holidays, Majeika.'

'On their what, sir? Please, sir, what are holidays?'

'Well, Majeika,' answered the Worshipful Wizard, *'holidays are a time when Britlanders go off in the rain and pretend that the sun is shining. If the sun does shine, they lie down in it and get all red and flaky, and pretend that they're turning an elegant shade of brown. They fight for space on crowded beaches and pretend they're all by themselves on a desert island. They chuck all sorts of awful drinks called Vino Cheapo down their throats and pretend that they like it. They spend hours and hours in airports, waiting to get on cramped planes, and pretend that they enjoy travel. And then they come back and say how wonderful it's been.'*

'Really, sir?' asked Mr Majeika. 'Are they quite mad, sir?'

'Quite mad, Majeika. But nothing will stop them doing it, year after year.'

'How very strange, sir. I'll never get the hang of these Britland folk.'

'Have a pleasant holiday, Mr Potter,' called Bunty Brace-Girdle through gritted teeth, as Mr Potter rode off on his motor cycle.

'Bye, Mr Potter!' called Hamish, waving. 'Now,' and he turned to Bunty. 'Where's the chockies?'

Mrs Brace-Girdle glared at Hamish. 'Chockies, Hamish Bigmore? There aren't going to be any chockies for you this holiday, my lad. Now, go and get a garden fork and start digging!'

Thomas and Melanie looked at each other, and while Melanie's mother was occupied in setting Hamish to work, they slipped off to look for Mr Majeika.

'And how are you going to spend your holidays, Mr Majeika?' they asked him, when they found him, still standing forlornly in the middle of the village street.

Mr Majeika sighed. 'I've no idea,' he said. 'Aren't you going away like everyone else?'

Melanie shook her head. 'Mummy says she's too busy. She says we can have one day at the seaside if we behave ourselves, but the rest of the time we've got to stay at home. It's dreadfully boring.'

'Maybe I could come round and cheer you up?' said Mr Majeika hopefully.

'Hamish Bigmore is staying with us,' said Thomas gloomily.

Mr Majeika's face fell. 'Maybe I won't come round after all,' he said.

'Come on,' announced Melanie briskly. 'I've got a little pocket-money left from last week. I'll buy us all ice-creams.'

When they got to the Cherry Tree Tea Rooms, they stopped and looked at a big notice in the window. 'Holiday Help Urgently Required. Apply Within.'

'Just look at that!' said Mr Majeika excitedly. 'The very thing!'

Thomas stared at him. 'You, Mr Majeika, help in the Tea Rooms?'

'It'd be something to do in the holidays,' answered Mr Majeika. 'Let's go and see.'

They went in. Mrs Cherry the proprietor was just coming out of the kitchen. 'Morning, kiddie-winkies,' she said to Thomas and Melanie. 'Know anyone, do you, who might help out here during the hols? I'm off for a couple of weeks and I need someone to run the place while I'm away.'

'Well,' said Thomas, 'Mr Majeika here . . .'

'. . . thinks he might,' continued Melanie.

'. . . manage to do it,' finished Thomas.

Mrs Cherry looked Mr Majeika up and down, taking an eyeful of his curious clothes, big owl-like glasses and odd mop-like hair. 'Well,' she said cautiously, 'he doesn't exactly look like the ordinary sort of waitress.'

'Never fear, Mrs Cherry!' chirped Mr Majeika,

taking a frilly apron off the back of a chair and putting it on. 'Help is at hand, Mrs Cherry. Just show me what to do.'

Mrs Cherry still looked doubtful. 'Well, Mr, er, Majorca, I suppose it's quite straightforward for anyone with a bit of British common sense. You'll soon get into the swing of things.' She went behind the counter and began to point things out to him. 'Up here we have the canister of Earl Barty Tea. Just add boiling water from this machine – and the other handle is for coffee.'

Shs turned several taps and steam began to gush out.

'Oh!' cried Mr Majeika delightedly, 'this is just like Walpurgis!'

'Yes?' said Mrs Cherry warily. 'Done much cooking before, have you, Mr Majorca?'

'Oh, just the occasional lizard stew, you know, Mrs Cherry.'

'You will have your little joke, Mr Majorca. Well, if you really think you can manage . . . I'm off tomorrow morning. See you then, at nine sharp, Mr Majorca.'

'At nine sharp, Mrs Cherry.'

At nine sharp the next morning, Mr Majeika rolled up on his trike at the Cherry Tree Tea Rooms. Thomas and Melanie were there to see him take over the business.

Ten minutes later, Mrs Cherry, who had given him the keys and final instructions, had disappeared down the road in her little open-top car. 'Toodle pip!' she called to him.

Happily, Mr Majeika changed the sign on the tea-shop door to 'Open'. Then he and the children went inside. 'I hope the first customer will turn up soon,' he said.

The first customer was Mrs Brace-Girdle, pulling her wheeled shopping-basket, with Hamish Bigmore in tow, eating an enormous ice-cream. She was very cross because Hamish had managed to get her to buy him the ice even though he had behaved very badly in the shops. She decided that she needed a strong cup of tea if she was going to cope with Hamish for the rest of the morning.

Someone came out of the kitchen to take her order. To her surprise, she saw it was not Mrs Cherry, but Thomas and Melanie. 'What are you two doing here?' she snapped crossly.

'Just helping Mr Majeika, Mummy,' said Melanie.

'Mr Majeika?' asked Mrs Brace-Girdle, irritably.

Mr Majeika emerged from the kitchen, wearing the frilly apron. 'Holiday relief, Mrs Brace-Girdle,' he explained. 'What can I get you, Mrs Brace-Girdle?'

'Tea,' said Mrs Brace-Girdle, still bad-tempered. Really, that tiresome little fellow Majeika did get everywhere. 'And Hamish had better have a cup of tea too. It'll do him more good than that ice-cream.'

'Tea for two it shall be, Mrs Brace-Girdle,' cooed Mr Majeika, remembering a Britland song he had heard on his radio when it wasn't tuned to Walpurgis, 'and two for tea, Mrs Brace-Girdle.' He began to sing as he led her to the table.

Picture you upon my knee,
Tea for two and two for tea,
Can't you see how happy we will be?
Day will break, and I'll awake
And start to bake a sugar cake . . .

'Just tea will do,' said Mrs Brace-Girdle crossly.

Half an hour later, the Cherry Tree Tea Rooms were getting quite busy. Or at least, a lot of people were sitting at the tables, waiting to be served. Mr Majeika was out in the kitchen, trying to cook their orders. These Britland people did ask for such strange things. He wished that Thomas and Melanie were there to help him. Unfortunately Mrs Brace-Girdle had taken them home with her when she had finished her tea.

'Come along, now,' called an elderly lady, tapping her fingers impatiently on her table. 'I've been waiting for twenty minutes. Where's my egg on toast?'

'Oh – er – so sorry,' panted Mr Majeika. 'One egg on toast coming up.' He hurried out of the kitchen carrying a plate and plonked it down in front of the elderly lady. On it was a thoroughly burnt, unbuttered piece of blackened toast and on top of it was an uncooked egg still in its shell. The lady stared at it, glared at Mr Majeika, got to her feet, and walked out of the Tea Rooms, banging the door behind her so that the bell jangled.

'Oh dear,' muttered Mr Majeika. 'I wonder if I did something wrong?'

'Excuse me,' said Miss Lammastide, who was sitting at another table. 'I asked for a cream tea. Have you got any cream teas?'

'Yes, yes, of course – so sorry to keep you waiting, madam,' panted Mr Majeika, rushing into the kitchen and getting some cream out of the fridge. In a moment he was back in the Tea Rooms carrying a plate. 'A cream T,' he said. 'I do hope that's right.'

'Well, er,' said Miss Lammastide, 'it's not quite what I was expecting.' On the plate, Mr Majeika had drawn the letter T in whipped cream.

'Waiter!' snapped the tall thin lady in glasses. 'Service over here, my man! I asked for baked beans, and where *are* my baked beans, I'd like to know?'

'Coming up right away,' said Mr Majeika, flicking his tuft of hair. 'Or rather, coming down.'

A torrent of baked beans fell out of nowhere and covered the tall thin lady. 'Eeeugggghh!' she screamed, rushing out of the Tea Rooms.

'Nothing wrong, is there, Majeika?' asked the voice of the Worshipful Wizard about an hour later.

'Well, sir,' said Mr Majeika, sitting down in the kitchen of the Cherry Tree Tea Rooms and resting his head in his hands. 'Yes, sir, there is something wrong. Just about everything, in fact.' He started to sob with misery and exhaustion. Nothing had gone right all morning. All his customers had stormed out in fury, and they must be warning their friends, because now it was almost lunchtime and no one was coming into the Tea Rooms at all.

'I just don't seem to have got the hang of Britland food yet, sir,' sighed Mr Majeika. 'You couldn't possibly . . .?'

'Possibly what, Majeika?'

'Possibly send me a little help from Walpurgis, could you, sir?'

The Worshipful Wizard thought for a moment. *'I'm not sure quite what you have in mind, Majeika. Walpurgian cooking isn't quite to Britland taste, we usually find. What about Witch Stichwort? She's famous for her –'*

'Ditchwater dumplings, sir,' said Mr Majeika. 'Yes, sir, I remember them very well. But I don't think they'd go down a treat in Much Barty, sir.'

'Well, Majeika, leave it to me. I'll see what I can do.'

'Oh, thank you, sir.'

Mr Majeika changed the sign to 'Closed' and went and sat on the back step, staring at the sky, hoping that the Worshipful Wizard would send someone down very soon.

After a few minutes, sure enough he saw a black balloon coming down through the clouds. 'Hooray!' he called out. 'Thank you, sir! I wonder who it is!'

'You'll see, Majeika. You'll see.'

The balloon didn't look big enough to carry Witch Stichwort. In fact, as it came closer, Mr Majeika could see that there wasn't a wizard or a witch hanging on to it at all, only some sort of small object that was dangling from it by a string. Oh dear, had the Worshipful Wizard let him down?

The balloon floated right down to the Cherry Tree Tea Rooms and dropped its parcel into the chimney. Mr Majeika could hear whatever the thing was falling inside with a clunk. As the black balloon floated away again, he hurried indoors to see what it was.

In the fireplace was lying an old oil lamp, the sort that is shaped like a teapot. Mr Majeika looked at it in disappointment. Was it some kind of a joke? He felt very sorry for himself. How could he learn to cook Britland food with an old lamp?

'*Help arrived safely, has it, Majeika?*' said the Worshipful Wizard's voice.

Sadly, Mr Majeika picked the thing up. 'But it's just an old lamp, sir.'

'*Yes, Majeika, an old lamp. A very old lamp. And you know all about Walpurgian lamps, don't you, Majeika?*'

Mr Majeika thought for a moment. 'Not really, sir,' he said.

'*Use it wisely, Majeika. It's yours just till Mrs Cherry returns. Use it wisely. Bye for now!*' And with a chuckle, the voice of the Worshipful Wizard fell silent.

Miserably, Mr Majeika held up the lamp and looked at it closely. Then he nearly dropped it in surprise. Inside it he could see a tiny, filthy, raggedy little man, stretching and yawning as if he had just woken up from a long sleep.

Mr Majeika stared. Then a thought struck him. A Walpurgian lamp! Why, of course. Even in Walpurgis they have bedtime stories, and suddenly Mr Majeika remembered the tale of Aladdin. Quickly he gave the lamp a rub.

There was a puff of smoke, and suddenly the little man was standing in front of Mr Majeika – except that he wasn't little any more; he was full sized. However, he was still very dirty and raggedy, and he still looked half asleep.

'Oh no!' he muttered. 'Not again! That blinkin' lamp hasn't been rubbed again, has it?' He yawned and dropped down into a heap on the floor. Mr Majeika shook him awake again.

'Aren't you supposed to say, "Your wish is my command, O Master"?' he asked.

'Yeah, yeah,'said the dirty, raggedy man. 'But first, tell me the worst, squire. Where am I this time?' he sniffed. 'Do I detect a whiff of spicy Singapore? Or maybe is this a casbah in old Casablanca? A souk in the sunny Sahara?'

Mr Majeika shook his head. 'I'm afraid not,' he said. 'Just the Cherry Tree Tea Rooms in Much Barty.'

'Wot!' cried the raggedy man, appalled. 'Not beastly old Britland? I'm an exotic kind of guy, I deserve better 'n this.'

'What I want to know,' said Mr Majeika, 'is whether you can cook?'

'Cook?' said the raggedy man. 'Me? No fear.'

'Then why in the name of Walpurgis did the Worshipful Wizard send you?'

'Search me, squire. Of course, though I can't cook, I can, at a pinch, *fetch* you any kind of food you want.'

'Fetch?' said Mr Majeika hopefully. 'Fetch absolutely anything from anywhere?'

'Well, of course, squire,' said the raggedy man. 'After all, I am – '

'A genie?' asked Mr Majeika eagerly.

'Got it in one, squire. So where'd you like me to start, then?'

The first thing the genie did – and he complained a lot, which the genie in *Aladdin* had never done – was to wash the dirty dishes. Or at least he stacked a great pile of them up in the kitchen and then just looked at them, with a magical look, and they became clean all by themselves.

'Mr Majeika!' Thomas and Melanie called from the doorway of the Tea Rooms. Mr Majeika left the genie and went to greet them.

'How are you managing, Mr Majeika?' Melanie asked him. 'We thought you might need a bit of help.'

'Thank you, said Mr Majeika, 'but I've got some help now.'

'What kind of help?' asked Thomas.

At that moment there was a great crash of breaking dishes from the kitchen, and a cry of 'Frizzling ferrets!'

Thomas's eyes became saucer-big. 'Is it – someone from Walpurgis?' he asked breathlessly. Mr

Majeika nodded. 'Another Wizard?' asked Thomas hopefully.

'Not exactly,' answered Mr Majeika. 'A genie.'

'Cor!' said the children.

They went into the kitchen so that the children could see the new arrival. 'He doesn't look much like a genie,' said Thomas in some disappointment.

'Genies,' added Melanie, 'usually dress in gold and jewels, not old rags.'

'And,' went on Thomas, dropping his voice to a whisper, 'he . . . *smells*.'

The genie heard him. 'So would you,' he snorted, 'if you'd been sloshing about in a paraffin lamp for five hundred years, with only an old wick for company.'

'Yes,' said Melanie soothingly, 'we understand. And I'm sure you're really a very genial genie, aren't you?'

'Nope,' said the genie grumpily. 'And my name's not Abanazar or any of that rubbish out of *Aladdin*, either. I'm called Jim.'

'Just Jim?' asked Melanie.

'Jim Genie. I've got a bruvver called Jeremy Genie and a sister called Geraldine Genie.'

'But how did you all become genies in the first place?' asked Thomas.

'Dunno,' said Jim Genie. 'Someone must have rubbed me family up the wrong way, I s'pose.' He turned to Mr Majeika. 'Well, squire? How'm I doing?'

Mr Majeika looked around the kitchen, which

was a good deal tidier. 'The place is a credit to you, Jim,' he said. 'But I wonder if, when you are waiting at the tables, you could do something about your . . .' He looked at Jim Genie's ragged appearance.

'Me clothes, squire? No bother. P'raps I could recommend me Dumb Waiter outfit, squire?' There was a flash, and suddenly Jim was dressed in a top hat and tail coat.

'That'll do nicely,' said Mr Majeika.

'You ain't seen nothing yet, squire. Now – ' And Jim took off his top hat with a sweeping gesture, twirled it in the air and chucked it into a corner of the Tea Rooms. There was another flash, a puff of smoke, a fountain of sparkles and suddenly out of nowhere appeared a three-piece orchestra of Wizards, playing tinkly music.

'Golly!' said Thomas.

'Well, well,' said Mr Majeika. 'That should do the trick.'

It did indeed. Within an hour, word had got round Much Barty that the Cherry Tree Tea Rooms could now boast a three-piece orchestra and was advertising that it could serve any kind of food the customer might order, however exotic: 'Temporarily Under New Management. Majeika's Magical Menu,' said the sign.

Soon there was a long queue stretching out on to the village green. Among the customers were two of the ladies who had been so angry with Mr Majeika that morning, Miss Lammastide and the thin lady in glasses, who was called Miss Gosling. In view of the notice, and the orchestra, they thought they would give the Tea Rooms another try. Even Bunty Brace-Girdle was curious to see what was going on, so she dragged Hamish Bigmore away from his deckchair and a mammoth box of chockies and took him down to the Tea Rooms.

Of course, Hamish pushed his way to the front of the queue, and had soon barged in and got a table. Reluctantly, knowing what he might do if she didn't keep an eye on him, Mrs Brace-Girdle followed him.

'Me first!' yelled Hamish, when Jim Genie in his top hat and tails came out of the kitchen to take customers' orders. 'I'm always first! And I want the biggest, creamiest cake in the place!'

Mr Majeika and Jim exchanged a glance, and Mr Majeika nodded. 'Coming up right away,' announced Jim. Mr Majeika gave a flick of his tuft, and suddenly there was the biggest and creamiest cake in the world – hitting Hamish Bigmore smack in the face.

From the kitchen, Thomas and Melanie roared with laughter. Meanwhile, Jim was taking orders from the other tables. 'One smoked trout, please,' said Miss Gosling.

In a moment, Jim had brought it from the kitchen – a big silvery trout on a plate, smoking a cigarette. Miss Gosling stared at it in amazement.

Jim consulted his order pad. 'Now, what else was it you all wanted, ladies? One Welsh Rabbit.'

He flicked his hand, and there on a plate sat a large floppy-eared rabbit wearing a tall Welsh hat. 'And one toad in the hole.' Miss Gosling gave a little scream, for there on the plate in front of her was a little mound of earth and moss, with a hole in the middle out of which peered two beady eyes.

'Have a nice meal, ladies,' said Jim. 'Now, who's next to order in this wizard little eaterie?'

At the end of the day, the takings were pretty wizard too. Jim had got the hang of things, and was now coming up with some delicious dishes. Thomas and Melanie counted up the money. 'Just look at that!' said Thomas. 'Loadsa money, isn't it?'

'You're a success all right!' said Melanie.

'Am I?' asked Mr Majeika. 'Are we? Well, I suppose we are. We're a success, Jim. Jim . . .? Where are you, Jim?' The genie was nowhere to be seen.

Anxiously, the children searched everywhere. Then Thomas had the bright idea of looking in the lamp. 'There he is!' he said. 'Curled up inside and fast asleep.'

'I'm not surprised,' said Mr Majeika. 'Poor chap, he has worked very hard.'

The next day the queues were bigger than ever, and once again Hamish Bigmore pushed his way to the front. This time he ordered a giant Ice-Cream Soda, and Mr Majeika told Jim not to pour it all over him – 'The other customers might expect to be treated the same way.' So Hamish was allowed to eat his ice-cream in peace.

When he had finished it, he began to poke around in his usual nosy way, and Thomas found him peering at Jim Genie's lamp, which was sitting on the mantelpiece among the horse brasses and other knick-knacks. 'Cor,' Hamish was saying, 'a real Aladdin's lamp.'

'Geddoff,' said Thomas. 'It's not yours.'

Hamish stuck his tongue out at Thomas.

Later that afternoon, Hamish sneaked away from Mrs Brace-Girdle, who as usual was trying to make him help with the gardening, stole some money from the collecting box for Poor Brownies on the kitchen shelf and hurried off to the Cherry Tree Tea Rooms to get another mammoth Ice-Cream Soda. He was the last customer, and was still eating away when Mr Majeika put up the 'Closed' sign. Jim had already magicked himself back into his lamp, and everything was now quiet.

'Come along, Hamish,' said Mr Majeika briskly. 'Time to go home.'

Hamish didn't like being hustled. For some time he had had his eye on the old Aladdin's lamp which was standing on the table – he reckoned he might get a few quid for that at one of the local junk shops. So when Mr Majeika annoyed him by trying to hurry him out, he popped out a hand and tucked it under his coat without Mr Majeika seeing.

* * *

Next morning, Mr Majeika was up bright and early at the windmill, eating his nettle yoghurt and looking forward to a busy day at the Tea Rooms.

'So everything's rubbing along nicely, is it, Majeika?' inquired the voice of the Worshipful Wizard.

'Oh, yes, sir, couldn't be better.'

'An ingenious genie, is he?'

'Oh, very, sir, thank you, sir.'

In a few moments, Mr Majeika had triked down to the main street of Much Barty and unlocked the door of the Tea Rooms. 'Good morning, Jim!' he called. 'I hope you slept well.' There was no reply, but Mr Majeika supposed Jim was fast asleep in the lamp as usual. He went to get it off the mantelpiece.

But the Walpurgian lamp was missing! Mr Majeika couldn't believe his eyes. Had Jim wandered off all by himself in the night? Impossible! Genies have to do as they are ordered and anyway, Jim was far too lazy to go off on a jaunt. Someone must have stolen it!

Mr Majeika rushed out of the Tea Rooms and into the village street. He thought he should call the police – but would the police believe him if he told them that a magic lamp had gone missing, with a genie inside it? They'd think he was mad. No, he had to try to find it himself.

'Nothing wrong, is there, Majeika?' asked the Worshipful Wizard in his ear.

'Wrong, sir? Oh, no, sir, good galaxies, no!' Mr Majeika remembered the Worshipful Wizard's warning: *'Use it wisely . . . It's yours just till Mrs*

Cherry returns.' What would Walpurgis say if he admitted to having lost it – *and* the genie who lived in it?

Mrs Brace-Girdle had decided that today she would take the children on the seaside trip she had promised them. As usual, she was bossing everyone about.

'Come along, kiddiewinks! Aren't we lucky we've such sunny weather for building sand-castles? Now, Melanie, look in the fridge and you'll find a quarter of a pound of pressed tongue for the sandwiches. And Thomas, please will you mash up some sardines.'

'Yuck,' muttered Thomas to himself.

'I'd much rather stay here and sneak off to the Tea Rooms,' whispered Melanie.

'Hamish!' called Mrs Brace-Girdle. 'Where are you? I want you to carry the hamper.'

There was a flopping noise and Hamish Bigmore came down the stairs into the kitchen. He was dressed in a swimming costume with rubber flip-pers, a rubber ring, and a snorkel. 'Cripes!' said Thomas. 'What's this? Something that Jaws sicked up?'

Hamish was carrying a towel rolled up under his arm. If Thomas and Melanie had looked closely, they would have seen something wrapped in the towel: a hard, shiny brass object inside which (though Hamish didn't know it) a certain person was fast asleep.

Hamish had already decided it was too risky

trying to sell the lamp – he had never thought of rubbing it – and he was taking it to the seaside so he could throw it away somewhere out of sight. Something told him that the lamp was rather important to Mr Majeika, and Hamish didn't want to risk being found with it in his possession in Much Barty. And he certainly had no intention of giving it back.

Mr Majeika was hurrying down the village street, casting his eyes about for anywhere that he might just possibly find the missing lamp. Suddenly he came to a shop with the sign 'Barty Antiques'. And there in the window it was! Yes, an absolutely identical lamp! His lamp! It must be, there couldn't be two like it.

He pushed open the door and went in. 'Can I help you?' asked the proprietor.

'I'd like to have a look at that lamp,' panted Mr Majeika, pointing at it. 'I think it's been stolen from the Tea Rooms.'

'Not very likely,' said the proprietor icily. 'We don't deal in stolen property here, I'll have you know. And how can you tell it was *that* lamp, and not these?' He pointed to a shelf at the back of the shop. On the shelf stood twenty more lamps, all looking exactly like Jim Genie's.

'Oh dear!' sighed Mr Majeika. What was he going to do? It was going to be a busier day than ever at the Tea Rooms. He'd got the Old Tyme Twinset Dancers booked in at four o'clock for a high tea and a hotpot, and he couldn't possibly cook for them without Jim – he knew everything would go wrong if he tried to cope himself. And what on earth was the Worshipful Wizard going to say?

At last the Brace-Girdle car got packed and Thomas, Melanie and Hamish were on their way to Barty Bay, with Mrs Brace-Girdle at the wheel.

'There's something suspicious about Hamish,' whispered Melanie to Thomas in the back of the car.

'Suspicious?' whispered Thomas. 'I don't know about suspicious, he's just a downright crook, we all know that.'

'Yes, but today he's looking extra specially fishy. I think he's got something hidden under that towel, he's carrying it very carefully. When we get to the seaside, let's sneak a look.'

Half an hour later, they had reached the seaside, and Mrs Brace-Girdle had put up her deckchair on the sand and got out her knitting. 'Now, children,' she announced firmly, 'we'll have the picnic a little later. Meanwhile off you go with your buckets and spades while Mummy gets on with knitting some nice blanket squares for the poor people.'

Thomas and Melanie followed Hamish Bigmore across the sands. Hamish got to some rocks near the water's edge, put down his towel, and advanced towards the sea. 'Now's our chance,' whispered Melanie.

'Wait till he gets in the water,' said Thomas.

'Not much hope of that. Look!' And Melanie

pointed to where Hamish had tripped over his own flippers and was flat on his face in the sand. He tried to get up, but only fell flat again.

Thomas started to laugh. 'Ssh!' said Melanie. 'Come on!' And while Hamish was distracted by his own troubles, they crept up to his towel and felt inside it.

'I thought so,' said Thomas, pulling out the lamp. 'The little . . . And how do you suppose Mr Majeika is managing without Jim Genie?'

'Come on,' whispered Melanie, 'let's take it over to that breakwater. We can be out of sight of Hamish and Mummy there.'

They took the lamp across the beach. 'Won't your mum be surprised if Jim Genie suddenly appears?' asked Thomas. 'She'll send him packing and warn us not to talk to strangers.'

'Yes,' said Melanie. 'Maybe we'd better leave Jim in the lamp till we get back to Much Barty.'

'But Mr Majeika needs him right away,' said Thomas. 'And maybe Jim will be able to get back there, just like that, if we wake him up. Genies can travel everywhere by magic.'

'Tell you what,' said Melanie, 'suppose we bury the lamp in the sand – we could make a sandcastle and hide it inside. Then if we put a hand in and rub the lamp, and Jim wakes up, he'll still be inside the sandcastle, and hidden from Mummy and Hamish, and we can think up some sort of plan with him.'

The idea worked very well. In a few minutes they had built a castle around the lamp. Thomas put his hand inside and rubbed it, and suddenly Jim's head appeared out of the top of the castle.

'Cor,' he spluttered, 'that yellow dust don't half get up one's nose.' He looked round. 'Oy, where am I? This ain't the Cherry Tree Tea Rooms, not unless the roof 'as blown orf?'

Thomas and Melanie explained what had happened. 'Nicked by Hamish Bigmore, eh?' said Jim. 'That little lad deserves to be smothered in ice-cream. But what are we going to do about it?'

'Can't you just take yourself back to the Tea Rooms by magic?' asked Melanie.

'Course I can ,' said Jim, 'if you tells me to. But once I gets there, I can't take orders from Apprentice Wizard Majeika.'

'Why not?' asked Thomas.

''Cause it's you what's rubbed the blinkin' lamp, son,' said Jim, 'an' I has to obey whoever wakes me up. If you wants me to work for Apprentice Wizard Majeika again, you'll have to let me get back to sleep in the lamp, give him the lamp, and then let *him* rub me awake.'

'And then you'll work for him again?' asked Melanie.

'Course I will,' said Jim. 'Mind you, I'd rather get me beauty sleep, but then "Your Wish Is My Command" and all that sort of rubbish.'

Mrs Brace-Girdle had set out the tongue and sardine sandwiches and was just about to call the children when she heard a voice on the Marine Parade behind her. 'Yoo-hoo, Bunty!'

She turned. 'Why, Mr Potter. Enjoying your holiday?'

Although it was a very hot day, Mr Potter was wearing his motor-cycle clothes and goggles. 'Not altogether, Bunty,' he said. 'Mrs Laburnum's semolina and cold beef has got a little too monotonous this year. And she keeps ticking me off for putting sand on the bathroom floor. Sand! How can I help it, when I've been paddling all morning without my shoes and socks?'

'Poor Mr Potter. So are you going home early?'

'I am going to return to Much Barty for just one night, and then I shall visit an old uncle of mine who lives at Malvern Spa.'

'Have you had lunch, Mr Potter?'

'Well, now that you mention it, dear lady, I have not. The final dose of semolina was too much for me.'

'Do join us for our picnic,' said Mrs Brace-Girdle. 'I'm sure the children can be persuaded to give up one or two of the tongue and sardine sandwiches.'

'Tongue!' cried Mr Potter rapturously. 'Sardines! Bunty dear, this is *haute cuisine* indeed.'

When Thomas and Melanie heard that Mr Potter was going back to Much Barty, they couldn't believe their luck. Fortunately, Hamish Bigmore had not yet come across the beach to have his lunch. He was still finding it very hard to stand upright in his flippers.

'Mr Potter,' said Melanie cautiously, 'when you get back to the village, do you think you could pop

71

round to the Cherry Tree Tea Rooms and give – something – to Mr Majeika?'

'But of course,' said Mr Potter. 'What is it, my dear? A nice stick of seaside rock? A bucket and spade?'

'You'll see, Mr Potter,' said Thomas. 'We'll put it in your motor-bike sidecar after lunch.'

Hamish was very cross that the lamp had disappeared, but when he glared angrily at Thomas and Melanie, they stared back furiously at him, and he realized that if he started to complain, he would have to admit where he had got the lamp in the first place.

He did not see Thomas putting the lamp in the sidecar, nor hear him reminding Mr Potter to take it to Mr Majeika as soon as he got back.

When the Brace-Girdle car reached Much Barty and drove down the village street, Thomas and Melanie could hear the orchestra playing in the Cherry Tree Tea Rooms. Once again there was a long queue outside.

'He got back all right, Melanie,' whispered Thomas, smiling.

At that moment, Jim Genie was serving a table-full of elderly ladies who had asked for ham. They were a little surprised when Jim came back to their table with a live pig under his arm. 'I just wondered whether you'd like it on or off the bone, ladies?' he asked.

* * *

After that, everything went like magic at the Tea Rooms until Mrs Cherry turned up, back from her holidays. 'My, my,' she said to Mr Majeika when she looked in the till, 'you *have* done well, Mr Majorca.'

'Me and Jim, Mrs Cherry,' said Mr Majeika. 'Especially Jim.'

Mrs Cherry eyed the strange-looking person in the top hat and tail coat. 'Friend of yours, Mr Majorca?' she asked.

'He's my genie, Mrs Cherry,' explained Mr Majeika.

'His genial acquaintance,' butted in Melanie hastily.

'Time to go, Jim,' said the voice of the Worshipful Wizard to Jim Genie, just as he and Mr Majeika were tidying up the kitchen for the last time.

'Oh, sir, do I have to? I'm just starting to enjoy myself.'

'Sorry, Jim. Into your lamp.'

Jim sighed. 'So long, then, squire,' he said to Mr Majeika, pulling noses with him in a Walpurgian goodbye. The children gave him a hug.

'You don't smell now,' said Melanie. 'It must be all that sea air.'

'Ready for lift-off,' announced Jim, grasping the lamp, and there was a flash and a puff of smoke and Jim and the lamp disappeared.

Mrs Cherry came into the kitchen. 'Your friend gone already, Mr Majorca? What a pity. I was going to offer him a job. By the way, Mr Majorca,

I brought you back a little present from the Costa del Sol.' She handed Mr Majeika a pair of Spanish castanets.

'I think you play them,' whispered Thomas, as Mr Majeika examined them in a puzzled way. 'They make a sort of clicking noise, and people dance to them.'

But it was too late. Mr Majeika had already bitten into the castanets. 'Delicious,' he said to Mrs Cherry, chewing hard.

So you've had a restful little holiday, then, Majeika?' inquired the Worshipful Wizard that night, as Mr Majeika was climbing into his hammock in his nightshirt.

'I wouldn't put it quite like that, sir,' yawned Mr Majeika. 'Quite exhausting really, sir. But fun. How's Jim, sir?'

'Back home and tucked up snug. He likes his sleep, does Jim. Mind you, he seems to have enjoyed himself. He's even put in a request to return to Much Barty.'

'Oh, sir? That's nice of him.'

'But he wants to have a rest first.'

'I see, sir. How long for?'

'Oh,' chuckled the Worshipful Wizard, *'about two hundred years.'*

3

HAPPY 232nd BIRTHDAY
TO YOU

It was a bright, breezy morning and Mr Majeika stepped out of the windmill in a very happy mood. Just the right sort of weather for the very special day that today happened to be.

The postman ought to be here soon, he thought, but he was too excited to wait. He got out his trike and pedalled off down the lane into Much Barty village. He reached the post office just as Mr Pulsford the postman was setting off on his rounds, with the bag of letters and parcels on the front carrier of his bicycle. Mr Majeika longed to say: 'What have you got for me today, Postman Pulsford? I bet there's heaps and heaps and heaps of letters and cards.' But he thought the postman might be cross if he tried to jump the queue, so to speak, rather than waiting his turn. So, at a little distance, he began to follow the postman on his rounds.

In about ten minutes, Postman Pulsford had visited School Cottage to deliver Mr Potter's letters and had pushed all sorts of important-looking envelopes through Councillor Mrs Brace-Girdle's front door. It was the windmill next, Mr Majeika knew. So he overtook Postman Pulsford, hurrying ahead of him and waiting on the stile at the bottom of Windmill Lane.

Yes, here came Postman Pulsford. He saw Mr Majeika, greeted him with a cheery 'Good morning!' – and went on down the main road without giving him anything.

Mr Majeika couldn't believe his eyes. 'Er, Mr Postman?' he called.

Postman Pulsford turned. 'Yes?' he asked cheerily.

'Haven't you forgotten something?' asked Mr Majeika. 'There must be some cards for me?'

Postman Pulsford shook his head. 'Nothing today, my friend.'

Mr Majeika's jaw dropped. 'But – perhaps you don't know my name? It's Majeika, spelt M – A – J – E –'

'I know your name all right, Mr Majeika,' said the postman. 'But there's no post for you today, I'm afraid.'

'No post at all?' said Mr Majeika unbelievingly. 'No parcels? No little packets? Not a single envelope?'

'Nothing, I'm afraid, Mr Majeika. Expecting something, were you?'

'Yes,' said Mr Majeika miserably. 'You see, it's my . . . Oh, never mind.' And he climbed sadly off the stile and went slowly up the lane. 'Not so much as a card,' he muttered to himself. 'Not so much as a box of Black Maggot chocs. *Someone* might have remembered . . .'

He fetched his books for school, came back down the lane, got on the trike and pedalled slowly into the village. It was certainly a lovely morning, but all the fun had gone out of life for Mr Majeika.

He triked very slowly past the post office, in the hope that Postman Pulsford, who should have got back from his round by now, might suddenly have discovered a whole lot of cards and parcels addressed to Mr Majeika. But there was no sign of the postman.

However, the door of the post office opened and out came Thomas and Melanie, sharing a bag of gob-stoppers they'd just bought. 'Morning, Mr Majeika,' they called.

'Good morning,' said Mr Majeika, making it sound as if it was a very bad morning.

'Whatever's the matter?' asked Melanie.

'Nothing, said Mr Majeika, sounding as if he was about to burst into tears. 'You'd just think that someone . . . in Walpurgis . . . would have . . . remembered.'

'Remembered, Mr Majeika?' asked Thomas. 'Remembered what?'

'Nothing,' said Mr Majeika gloomily. 'Now, children, hurry along to school, mustn't be late.' And he pedalled off, looking a picture of misery.

Thomas and Melanie looked at each other. 'D'you know what?' said Thomas. 'He looks like someone's who's miserable because . . .'

'. . . because,' said Melanie, 'everyone has forgotten his birthday.'

Thomas nodded. 'That's just what I thought.'

Up in Walpurgis, someone *had* remembered. Mr Majeika's Aunty Bubbles, a jolly old witch who always dressed in a striking costume of blackbird and raven feathers, knew all about it and at this moment she was jogging the memory of the Worshipful Wizard himself.

'Your Worshipfulness,' she was saying, 'you haven't forgotten what day it is?'

The Worshipful Wizard sighed and reached for a big heavy book bound in leather. 'Somebody's birthday, no doubt,' he said. 'It's always somebody's birthday.'

In fact it wasn't always somebody's birthday in Walpurgis, because Walpurgians only have birthdays once every forty-seven years. And this meant that people were always forgetting when someone's birthday did come around, because forty-seven years is a long time to remember. So when a Walpurgian said coyly to another Walpurgian, 'You haven't forgotten what day it is?', this always meant that a birthday had come round at last and everyone had forgotten it.

'Let me see,' said the Worshipful Wizard, opening his book, which said *Birthdays* on the front. 'Birthday of Mantovani . . . Birthday of Macchiavelli . . .' He turned a page. 'Good galaxies! Is it really the birthday of . . .?'

Aunty Bubbles smiled and nodded, showing her

alternate black and white teeth. 'The birthday of a little nephew of mine, sir. Down in Britland.'

When Mr Majeika got to school, he was astonished to see Mr Potter standing at the gates dressed in long flowing robes and carrying a gigantic fork.

'Ah, Majeika!' beamed Mr Potter. 'It's a very special day today. You haven't forgotten, I hope?'

Mr Majeika was all smiles. 'No, Mr Potter, *I* haven't forgotten, though I thought everyone else had. It's – '

'That's right,' said Mr Potter. 'It's the Much Barty Well Dressing Day.'

' – my birthday,' said Mr Majeika, but Mr Potter wasn't listening.

'Yes, Majeika, Well Dressing Day. The day upon which the entire village gives thanks to our Much Barty Well for its crystal clear waters, which for many centuries supplied our little community with all it needed for drinking and washing. Come and see!'

He led Mr Majeika across to the edge of the village green, where there stood a moss-encrusted old well with a wooden bucket. Nobody ever used it these days – the little water it contained was all green and slimy – but Councillor Mrs Brace-Girdle had discovered about Well Dressing Day in a local history book, and she made everyone perform the ceremony each year dressed up in ridiculous costumes.

'There will be an Aquatic Tableau, Majeika,' explained Mr Potter. 'Hence my own costume, which you will have recognized as Neptune, god of the sea.' He brandished his gigantic fork in the air; Mr Majeika wondered how it was possible to eat anything with it. 'The Ladies' Circle, led of course by Mrs Brace-Girdle,' went on Mr Potter, 'will be appearing as Water Nymphs, and the climax of the event will be the entry of the god Pan, played on this occasion by Hamish Bigmore. All in all, Majeika, I think I can promise you a very special day.'

'Yes, Mr Potter,' said Mr Majeika hopefully. 'In fact, a real . . . birthday treat, sir?'

Thomas and Melanie were waiting at the school gate when Mr Majeika came back with Mr Potter. 'Mr Majeika,' whispered Melanie. 'Something tells us it's your . . .'

'. . . birthday!' whispered Thomas.

Mr Majeika's eyes brightened up and he nodded. 'This very day,' he whispered.

'See you at the Well Dressing Ceremony, Majeika,' said Mr Potter, who hadn't heard any of this. He went off to School Cottage to open his letters.

'How old are you, Mr Majeika?' asked Thomas.

'Thomas!' said Melanie disapprovingly. 'You shouldn't ask grown-ups their age.'

'It's only mums over thirty who keep it a secret, silly,' said Thomas.

'I'm two hundred and thirty-two, Thomas,' said Mr Majeika proudly.

'Gosh!' said Thomas and Melanie.

'Give or take the odd full moon,' added Mr Majeika.

'Cor,' said Thomas, 'that makes you even older than Mr Potter.'

'But why are you looking so sad, Mr Majeika?' asked Melanie. 'Birthdays are happy occasions here in Britland.'

'They're happy occasions in Walpurgis, too,' said Mr Majeika miserably, 'except when nobody remembers them.'

Up in Walpurgis, Aunty Bubbles had not only remembered Mr Majeika's birthday; she had spent days and days wrapping his presents, tying them neatly in the very best quality black cobwebs. She had them all piled up and ready now, and she was asking a special favour of the Worshipful Wizard.

'Now, I'm very much aware, Your Worshipfulness,' she was saying to the venerable bearded figure, 'that my nephew's just one of many little banished Wizards down there in Britland and other parts of the globe. But after all, Your Worshipfulness, he is very far from home, poor dear. And Walpurgians only get a birthday once every forty-seven years. So I was wondering, Your Worshipfulness, if I mightn't – just this once – pop down there myself, Your Worshipfulness.'

The Worshipful Wizard lifted his enormous white eyebrows. 'Pop down, Aunty Bubbles? To Britland? My dear venerable Witch, have you ever been to Britland before?'

Aunty Bubbles nodded. 'It was just after I'd

gained my Solo Broomstick Flying Licence, Your Worshipfulness. It was in the reign of King Henry the Eighth of Britland, if I remember rightly.'

'But that was a very long time ago, Aunty Bubbles,' remarked the Worshipful Wizard, shaking his head. 'And perhaps you're not quite as spry on a broomstick as you used to be?'

'Maybe not, Your Worshipfulness. But I can't bear to think of him being all alone. Not on his birthday, Your Worshipfulness.'

The Worshipful Wizard thought for a moment. 'I'll tell you what,' he said. 'Seeing as it's such a special occasion, why don't we all pop down?'

Aunty Bubbles's eyes widened. '*All*, sir?'

'That's right,' said the Worshipful Wizard. 'All the Walpurgian Witches and Wizards – or at least any who want to come.'

The word spread quickly around Walpurgis that the Worshipful Wizard was taking a party down to Britland to celebrate Majeika's birthday. The news caused special excitement in the Witches' Knitting Circle.

'I says!' said a voice. 'What a simply spiffings idea.'

It was Wilhelmina Worlock.

Wilhelmina Worlock was a big fat ugly Witch who had been trying to marry Mr Majeika for years and years and years. The only reason Mr Majeika was glad to be banished to Britland was to escape from her. But recently she had come down to Much Barty and had been an awful nuisance, getting Mr

Potter to make her the music teacher at the school and trying all sorts of tricks with love potions to lure Mr Majeika into marrying her at last. He and Thomas and Melanie had only managed to send her back to Walpurgis with the greatest difficulty. Had they known that she was planning to come back to Much Barty on the birthday trip, they would have turned quite pale with alarm.

At the mid-morning break, Mr Majeika overheard Thomas and Melanie talking about him.

'It's such a shame,' Thomas was saying. 'You'd think someone would have remembered.'

'Of course,' said Melanie, 'the day isn't over yet. Maybe . . .?' They looked at each other. Mr Majeika knew he shouldn't be listening, but he did hope that they might come over to him and tell him they were going to organize a party or something.

Sure enough, they had got to their feet and were running excitedly towards him.

'Mr – ' called Thomas.

'Yes?' said Mr Majeika hopefully.

' – Potter!' called Thomas, running off towards School Cottage. 'Mr Potter!'

Mr Majeika's face fell. This was worse than ever. Thomas and Melanie knew about his birthday – and even they weren't going to do anything about it! He had never felt so miserable in his life.

'So you see,' Melanie was explaining to Mr Potter, 'it's his birthday and no one has sent him any presents or anything.'

'And we thought,' said Thomas, 'that everyone could organize a surprise party for him.'

'A party!' said Mr Potter. 'We could hold it after the Well Dressing Ceremony. What a perfectly jolly idea. But don't let him hear about it. It's got to be a real surprise.'

Mr Potter telephoned Mrs Brace-Girdle. 'A birthday party?' she said. 'What a top-hole idea. Who's it for?'

'Mr Majeika,' said Mr Potter.

'Oh,' said Mrs Brace-Girdle. '*Him*. Well, if you say so, Mr Potter. I'll let bygones be bygones and make a really spiffing cake.'

Mr Majeika came early out of school lunch; he didn't have any appetite. He wandered down the village street, to the post office, just in case . . . But when he asked, there were no parcels or letters for him.

Leaving the shop, he looked sadly at the displays of birthday cards. Maybe he should buy one for himself; then at least he would have one. But none of them was at all suitable – the ages were all wrong. 'Happy Fifth Birthday', 'Happy Sixth Birthday', and so on. There weren't any that had his age on them.

Then he saw the birthday badges. 'I am 5', 'I am 6', 'I am 7'. One of those would have been just the thing, he thought. People would see it and know that it was his birthday.

He thought for a moment, then flicked his tuft

of hair. One of the badges changed magically, so that now it read 'I am 232'.

'I'll have this one,' he said to Mrs Pulsford behind the counter.

Far too many Wizards and Witches wanted to come down from Walpurgis to Britland for Majeika's birthday party. The Worshipful Wizard was regretting his decision. He had to do something at once.

'Regrettably I have to inform you,' he announced, 'that invitations to Majeika's party today must be strictly limited.'

There was a groan of disappointment.

'Limited,' he went on, 'to those who attended Majeika's last birthday party, which was in 1942. And they are – ' he examined a list, ' – his best friend at Sorcery School, Wizard Spells; his Wand Polisher, Wizard Spitt; his Aunty Bubbles; and of course, myself.'

'But what about mees?' said a voice.

'You are not included, Wilhelmina Worlock.'

'But,' spluttered Willy Worlock, 'I'm his long lost loves, Your Worshipfulness. And I've put glitter on me warts, speciallys for the party.'

'You heard what he said,' Aunty Bubbles told Miss Worlock. 'You ain't going.'

Willy Worlock burst into tears and hit Aunty Bubbles with her fan.

Class Three and the rest of the St Barty's School children filed out on to the village green for the

Well Dressing Ceremony. They were all looking embarrassed and cross on account of their ridiculous costumes: the girls were dressed as Flower Fairies and the boys as Tree Sprites, with headdresses made of twigs.

Mr Majeika arrived just in time to join the end of the line. He looked down proudly at his 'I am 232' badge.

'And now,' announced Mr Potter, when they had arrived at the well. 'I would like to welcome you to the St Barty's School Well Dressing and Aquatic Tableau. As usual, we shall begin by singing the Well Dressing Song, composed in Victorian times by Lady Maud Barty and sung every year since then.' He handed out the copies of the words, and everyone began to sing.

> O Aqua, dear,
> We're gathering here
>   To keep your waters flowing.
> Our Water Nymphs
> You soon will glimpse;
>   Their chests are overflowing.

As he sang, Mr Potter glanced up into the sky, hoping that the rain would keep off. He spotted a small black cloud moving rather fast, but it did not look big enough to mean rain.

It was not a black cloud; it was the party from Walpurgis, descending at top speed to Much Barty. Several of them, including the Worshipful Wizard himself, had not flown for a long while, and they were not enjoying the experience. Wizard

Spitt was coming down head first, while Aunty Bubbles was descending at such a speed that the wind had blown out her bloomers like black balloons.

Down on the village green, Mr Potter led the children in the second verse.

> O Aqua, dear,
> Keep flowing clear,
>   And trickle on throughout the year.
> We bring you Flox,
> And Ladysmocks,
>   To keep your droplets glowing.

Several Flower Fairies advanced with bunches of wildflowers. Mr Potter looked hopefully at his watch; it would soon be over, thank goodness. Not a very big audience this year. In fact the only person sitting in the rows of chairs opposite the well was Postman Pulsford, and he seemed to have gone to sleep.

Mr Potter cleared his throat. 'I think it's time for the Water Nymphs to step forward,' he announced. But there was no sign of the Water Nymphs; they must still be dressing at Mrs Brace-Girdle's cottage. 'Well then,' continued Mr Potter rather desperately, 'while we, er, wait for the Water Nymphs, maybe our personification of the Greek god Pan would like to blow us a few notes on his merry little pipes?'

But the Greek god Pan was not there either. 'The

Greek god Pan,' explained Mr Potter, 'will be played by Hamish Bigmore . . . When he gets here.'

The Greek god Pan was just coming out of the post office clutching an enormous box of chocolates. He had not wanted to play the part of Pan, and the goatskin trousers and mock tail were the silliest things he had ever had to wear in his life. He had sneaked off to the post office to buy some chockies to get up his strength for the ordeal. Hamish Bigmore did not like being laughed at, and he knew the rest of the school were going to laugh when they saw him as the Greek god Pan.

'Ouch!' cried the Wizards and Witches, landing in a hedge just behind the post office. They picked the thorns and twigs out of their clothes and hair, and Aunty Bubbles adjusted her best hat – a bird's nest, with a live blackbird sitting on the eggs. She had made it specially for her nephew Majeika's birthday party.

'Here we are, then,' she cried enthusiastically. 'Much Barmy.'

'Don't you mean Much Barty?' corrected the Worshipful Wizard.

At that moment, Hamish Bigmore, dressed as the Greek god Pan, and stuffing chocolates into his mouth, walked past on the other side of the hedge. Wizard Spitt saw him.

'No,' he said. 'Aunty Bubbles is right. It's very definitely Much Barmy.'

* * *

'Ah, children, here at last are the Water Nymphs,' announced Mr Potter with relief. 'And how splendid they all look, don't they, children?'

The Water Nymphs – Mrs Brace-Girdle, Miss Lammastide, Miss Gosling and various other village ladies – certainly looked a sight, dressed in various left-overs from the Much Barty Operatic Society costume cupboard. They pranced around for a few minutes to the strains of a concertina, while the school children giggled. Mr Majeika looked on in amazement at this latest Britland oddity.

'And now,' announced Mr Potter. ''tis none other than the Greek god Pan. And doesn't he look exquisite?'

'Exquisite' was not quite the right word for Hamish Bigmore, who pranced unwillingly up to the well, scowling horribly. 'Play your little pipes, Hamish!' called Mr Potter. Hamish blew a shrieking blast and everyone covered their ears.

Everyone except Mr Majeika, who was feeling so miserable about his unremembered birthday that Hamish's dreadful pipe-playing scarcely caught his attention. So he didn't block his ears – which was why he, and no one else, heard a shriek from the edge of the village green.

'There he is! There he is! There's my little cheeky Majeeky!'

'Great galaxies!' muttered Mr Majeika. 'It's Aunty Bubbles!'

* * *

'*Come follow, follow, follow,*' Mr Potter was singing lustily, '*the merry, merry pipes of Pan!*'

Thomas nudged Melanie, 'Look!' he whispered.

Melanie looked. 'Gosh!' she whispered. 'Is it really – ?'

Thomas nodded. 'Walpurgians, Melanie. They didn't forget his birthday after all.'

No one else had seen them, and no one was likely to now, for Mr Potter had made everyone join hands and dance round the well, singing about the merry, merry Pipes of Pan. As for the Greek god Pan, he had eaten too many chockies. He leant over the well and was sick into it.

'Aunty Bubbles!' gasped Mr Majeika, rushing up to her in delight and amazement.

'Little nephew Majeeky!' crooned Aunty Bubbles, stretching out her talons to embrace him.

'B–but what in the name of Walpurgis are you doing here?' panted Mr Majeika. 'And in broad daylight, too?'

'What d'you think we're doing, nephew Majeeky?' said Aunty Bubbles happily. 'Come to celebrate your two hundred and thirty-second birthday, ain't we?'

Behind her, Mr Majeika saw the approaching figures of Wizard Spitt, Wizard Spells, and – yes! no less than the Worshipful Wizard himself.

'T–thank you all,' gasped Mr Majeika. 'I'm very h–honoured by this visit. B–but . . . it's going to cause a few p–problems.'

* * *

'This is going to cause a few problems,' muttered Melanie to Thomas. 'There's the surprise party that Mr Potter has got Mummy to lay on for him. Everyone will be terribly offended if he goes off with the Walpurgians.'

Thomas nodded. 'And he can't bring the Walpurgians to our surprise party,' he said, 'because then everybody would discover that he was a wizard, and nobody must ever know that. Whatever are we going to do, Melanie?'

'Let's ask him to shoo the Walpurgians somewhere out of sight,' said Melanie. 'Maybe the Bluebell Woods, just up the road?'

The two children slipped out of the dancing ring and across the green.

'Thomas and Melanie,' said Mr Majeika proudly when he saw them coming, 'I want you to meet my Worshipful Wizard.' Thomas and Melanie bowed and introduced themselves to the Worshipful Wizard. 'And this,' said Mr Majeika, 'is my Aunty Bubbles.'

Aunty Bubbles stepped forward and held out her talons to shake hands. 'Ever met a real Witch before, have you, children?' she asked.

Thomas nodded.

'Only the one,' said Melanie.

'Miss Wilhelmina Worlock,' said Thomas.

'Oh, *her*,' said Aunty Bubbles contemptuously. 'That dreadful old hag. Well, children, you won't be seeing her today.'

* * *

Up in Walpurgis, a fat figure was struggling with the dwarf whose job it was to guard the hole that led down to Britland.

'Whaddya mean, I haven't got an invitations?' she was hissing. 'Wilhelmina is the life and souls of any party, and she's going to this one – like it or nots!'

She elbowed the dwarf out of the way and jumped through the hole.

'Well, now,' Aunty Bubbles was saying happily to Thomas and Melanie, 'aren't you going to introduce us all to your other little friends, then? The ones who are singing and dancing over there?'

'What!' cried Mr Majeika. 'No, no, absolutely no, Aunty Bubbles.'

'Why ever not?' asked Aunty Bubbles, offended. 'Not ashamed of your old Aunty, are you?' The blackbird in her hat started to chirp noisily.

'Of course not,' said Mr Majeika. 'It's just that – *they* don't know that . . . they have no idea that . . . you . . . I . . .'

'The problem is,' explained Melanie, 'that Mr Potter the headmaster, and Councillor Mrs Brace-Girdle, who's my mother and one of the school governors, and Miss Lammastide and Miss Gosling and Hamish Bigmore over there – '

' – don't know,' continued Thomas, 'that Class Three's teacher, Mr Majeika here, is actually no ordinary schoolmaster, but a Failed Wizard of the Third Class Removed.'

'And if they found out,' said Melanie, 'he'd be

in trouble. Given the sack. Sent away. Booted out. Expelled.'

'Or worse still,' said Thomas, 'as they don't believe in Wizards and Witches, they'd think he was mad, and they'd lock him up in a hospital – and probably all of you too!'

'Oh dear,' said Mr Majeika gloomily. 'Would they really? I'd never thought of that.'

'So,' said Melanie firmly, 'we think you'd better have your surprise birthday party somewhere out of sight.'

Miss Wilhelmina Worlock came down to earth with a bump, among the bushes. 'Bloomin' Britlands,' she muttered angrily to herself. 'The things one does for loves.' She picked the twigs and thorns out of her clothes. 'What is this place? A bloomin' bluebell woods?'

'This is the Barty Bluebell Woods,' explained Melanie to the Walpurgians. 'We thought it would do nicely for your party.'

'Yes, dear, it will,' said Aunty Bubbles cheerily. 'Very nicely. Now, then – ' And she clapped her hands. Instantly a ring of broomsticks appeared in the middle of a clearing. Aunty Bubbles clapped her hands again, and the broomsticks were magically festooned with glistening cobwebs and lit by swinging lanterns. Another clap of the hands, and a table appeared in the middle of the ring, laden with birthday goodies.

'She's magical, Melanie!' breathed Thomas.

Aunty Bubbles patted him on the head. 'See, I hasn't lost my touch, has I? Even if I am eight hundred and twelve and a half.'

The Walpurgian party sat down happily at the table and began to tuck in. There were sandwiches of nettle and bogweed, and delicious little cakes of squashed beetle. At least, the Walpurgians thought they were delicious, but Thomas and Melanie only took a few little nibbles to be polite.

Suddenly Melanie clapped her hand to her mouth.

'What's the matter?' asked Thomas. 'Eaten too much bogweed, Melanie?'

'No, I've just remembered! Mr Majeika, you shouldn't be here at all – you should be at the surprise party!'

'Surprise party?' echoed Mr Majeika. 'But Melanie, *this* is a surprise party – a real surprise.'

'Surprises! Surprises!' screamed a voice from the trees behind them, and an enormous black-clad figure leapt into the clearing.

Oh *no!*' cried Thomas.

Mr Potter and Mrs Brace-Girdle, assisted by Miss Lammastide and Miss Gosling, had just finished setting out the plates for Mr Majeika's surprise birthday party in School Cottage.

'Wonderful,' said Mr Potter, looking around him happily. 'Now the only thing that's missing is Majeika.'

'Huh!' snorted Mrs Brace-Girdle. 'How like him to be late for his own party.'

* * *

94

'Wilhelmina!' Mr Majeika was saying in horror, gazing at the all-too-familiar figure of Willy Worlock, as she tucked into the nettle and bogweed sandwiches. 'Who in the name of Walpurgis invited *you*?'

'Wilhelmina Worlock,' said the Worshipful Wizard sternly, 'you were not given an invitation.'

'Pardonnez-moi, Your Worshipfulness,' spluttered Miss Worlock through a mouthful of sandwich, 'but you sees, I just couldn't resist the opportunity to gives my Majeika a birthday nibble, Your Worshipfulness. 'Cos I loves to nibbles my Majeika, Your Worshipfulness.'

'Don't let her!' cried Mr Majeika. 'Send her away!'

The Worshipful Wizard sighed. 'Wilhelmina Worlock, you have flagrantly disobeyed the rules. But I suppose that now you're here . . .'

'Oh, thank yous, Your Worshipfulness!' cried Wilhelmina in triumph. 'And now it's time for party games. Let's have a Walpurgian Kiss Chase, Your Worshipfulness!'

She made a dive for Mr Majeika, crying 'Kissy, kissy!'

'Oh, no!' yelled Mr Majeika, making a dive for the bushes.

The children ran after him, as did Wilhelmina, making horrible kissing noises with her pursed lips. 'Coming to gets you, Best Beloveds!' she crooned – and fell heavily into a ditch.

'Quick, Mr Majeika!' called Melanie. 'Now's

your chance to escape from her, *and* get to the other birthday party.'

In School Cottage, Mrs Brace-Girdle was just looking crossly at her watch when the door burst open, and there stood a very out-of-breath Mr Majeika, with Thomas and Melanie on either side of him.

'Ah, there you are at last, Majeika,' said Mr Potter. 'A little surprise for you. We want to wish you happy birthday with a real Barty Party.'

They all began to sing 'Happy Birthday To You.'

'Thank you, thank you!' said Mr Majeika. He was so happy that he felt like crying.

Outside School Cottage, Hamish Bigmore, still dressed as the Greek god Pan, could hear the singing, and was very angry. Mr Potter had forbidden him to come to the party after he was sick; he said what Hamish needed was fresh air and exercise, not more food. He told him to go for a run round the village green, and he had asked Postman Pulsford, who had come to the party, to guard the door and keep Hamish out.

Hamish had tried to push the front door open but Postman Pulsford held it fast. So Hamish was sulking in the front garden, kicking Mr Potter's roses.

Suddenly he heard a voice in the street. 'Coo-ee! Kissy, kissy! Where are you, Best Beloveds?'

Hamish Bigmore thought he recognized that voice. 'Miss Worlock!' he said in amazement.

Willy Worlock panted up the road, and in at the

gate of School Cottage. She looked at the Greek god Pan, and thought she recognized that face. 'Why, if it isn't Hamish Bigmouths! Have you seen my Best Beloveds?'

Hamish Bigmore nodded. 'He's in there,' he said, pointing at the front door. 'There's a party going on, but I'm not invited, Miss Worlock.'

'Ah,' said Miss Worlock, 'the same thing just happened to mees. But we'll soon put a stops to thats, won't we?'

In School Cottage, everyone had put on funny paper hats, and Mrs Brace-Girdle was handing round a plate of rock cakes that she had made specially for the party. But Thomas saw that Mr Majeika was looking worried.

'What's the matter?' he whispered.

'I don't want to offend poor Aunty,' explained Mr Majeika. 'Not to mention the Worshipful Wizard. They'll be terribly upset if they find I've slipped away from *their* party. Couldn't I go back there now?'

'You can't just walk out,' whispered Melanie, 'or my mummy will be absolutely furious. I don't know what we can do.'

'If only something surprising would happen,' muttered Thomas, 'to take people's attention away from you. Then you could just slip away.'

At that moment, there was an enormous crash. Wilhelmina Worlock had pushed the front door open, nearly flattening Postman Pulsford. 'Coo-ee!' she cried, bursting into the room, 'Kissy, kissy!'

'Oh no!' gasped Mr Majeika, heading for the window. 'Quick!' Thomas and Melanie helped him to climb out.

'Why, Miss Worlock,' beamed Mr Potter, holding out his arms in welcome. 'Back in Much Barty so soon? Do let me give you a cup of tea.'

'And where has my naughty nephew got to?' Aunty Bubbles was asking. 'He's taking an awfully long time on that Kiss Chase.'

'Ah, here he comes now,' said the Worshipful Wizard, as Mr Majeika panted into the clearing, followed by Thomas and Melanie. 'Just in time for the next course, Majeika.'

'The next course, sir?' gasped Mr Majeika, who was already feeling the effects of a plateful of rock cakes on top of nettle and bogweed sandwiches.

'That's right, my little Majeeky,' said Aunty Bubbles cheerily. 'This is where the party food really starts. There's Stuffed Legs of Lizards, Canapés of Caterpillars, and Ants in Aspic. All your favourites, I remember! And to follow that, the hot food. Beetle Bourguignon and Mole Marinière.'

'You've done all this for me?' said Mr Majeika weakly.

'And we mustn't forget the presents,' said the Worshipful Wizard, handing over a parcel wrapped in black crepe paper. 'Happy birthday, Majeika.'

'A present from you, sir?' gasped Mr Majeika, overwhelmed. 'Such an honour, sir!' He opened the parcel. 'Oh!' he cried delightedly. 'It's a – a bat!'

'Your very own pet, Majeika,' said the Worshipful Wizard. 'All Britlanders dote on pets, don't they, Majeika?'

'They certainly do, sir,' said Mr Majeika happily, stroking his bat. 'My very own pet!'

'My very owns pet!' screamed a voice, and Wilhelmina Worlock, still clutching a cup of tea from Mr Potter's party, bounded into the clearing. 'Kissy, kissy!'

'We've finished the Kiss Chase now, Wilhelmina,' announced the Worshipful Wizard firmly.

'Oh, haves we?' said Willy Worlock, very disappointed.

'You must get back to School Cottage, Mr Majeika,' whispered Melanie urgently. 'They'll be wondering where on earth you are.'

'What am I going to do?' muttered Mr Majeika desperately. Then his face suddenly brightened. 'I know!' he said. 'Come along, everyone,' he announced. 'Time for a game of Wizards' Buff! You remember the rules? You all put on blindfolds and you have to chase me! Off we go!'

At School Cottage, Mr Potter was organizing a game of Oranges and Lemons.

'Where on earth is Mr Majeika?' said Mrs Brace-Girdle crossly. 'He's vanished again.'

'Oh, don't you worry, Bunty,' said Mr Potter. 'You know Majeika. He's always there when you really need him – he just pops up like magic.'

At that moment, Mr Majeika climbed in through the window again, followed by Thomas and Melanie.

'Ah, there you are, Majeika,' said Mr Potter happily. 'Just in time for the games. Wizard party, eh?'

'You can say that again, Mr Potter,' panted Mr Majeika.

Wilhelmina Worlock was puffing up the road, like an outsize steam-engine. 'I'll teach yous, Best Beloveds! I'll teach yous to slip off from Willy when she's got her blindfold on. You know the rules of Wizards' Buff, Best Beloveds. When I catches yous, I has to give yous a smacking great kiss! Here I comes, Best Beloveds.'

'*Here comes a candle to light you to bed,*' Mr Potter was chanting, as everyone played Oranges and Lemons.

The door burst open and Wilhelmina Worlock thundered into the room. 'Cooee, Best Beloveds!' she cried.

Mr Majeika made a dive for the window.

'*And here comes a chopper to chop off your head!*' Down came the 'chopper' – the arms of Miss Lammastide and Miss Gosling – right on top of Willy Worlock, felling her to the floor.

'I – can't – run – any – further,' gasped Mr Majeika, as Thomas and Melanie dragged him into the clearing, where Aunty Bubbles was rearranging the table.

'Well, Majeika, I can see you're enjoying yourself,' said the Worshipful Wizard. 'And now it's time for something very special.'

'*My* birthday present to you, dearest nephew Majeeky,' said Aunty Bubbles.

'Your present, Aunty?' asked Mr Majeika, trying to get his breath back. 'Not more cobweb socks?'

Aunty Bubbles shook her head, and the plaits of her hair began to rise – everyone in the Majeika family could cast spells by wiggling their hair. There was a thunderclap and a puff of smoke, and suddenly in the middle of the table there appeared a gigantic many-tiered black birthday cake, lit by two hundred and thirty-two black candles.

'I baked it myself,' explained Aunty Bubbles. 'It's covered in your favourite beetle juice icing, and decorated with grubs glacé.'

'Two hundred and thirty-two candles, Melanie!' said Thomas in amazement.

'Now,' said Aunty Bubbles, 'who's going to be Aunty's big boy and sneeze out all his candles in two goes, eh?'

Mr Majeika drew in his breath, and gave an absolutely enormous sneeze. All the candles went out, except for a single one in the very middle. Everyone cheered and clapped.

'Well, now, Majeika,' announced the Worshipful Wizard,' 'as there is just one candle left, you are allowed something very special when you blow it out. A wish, Majeika.'

'A wish, sir?'

'One magical wish, Majeika. Is there something you'd like to wish for, Majeika? It's the only wish you'll be granted until your next birthday in forty-seven years' time. Think carefully, Majeika.'

'I don't need to think, sir,' said Mr Majeika. 'I know just what I want. It concerns Miss Worlock, sir.'

'Mees?' gasped a voice, as Wilhelmina Worlock galumphed into the clearing. 'Did he mention little mees? Oh, Aunty Bubbles, do you think he wants mees at last? D'you think he's finallys going to takes me off the shelf and dusts me down?'

'Well, Majeika?' asked the Worshipful Wizard.

'I wish,' said Mr Majeika solemnly, leaning over to the single candle in the middle of the birthday cake. 'I wish – not to see Wilhelmina Worlock again for a very long time!' And he blew out the candle.

'Whats!' shrieked Wilhelmina Worlock. 'You can'ts do this to me, Best Beloveds!' But it was too late. A magical gust of air plucked her up and shot her skywards through the branches, straight towards Walpurgis. 'But I'm your long lost loves, Best Beloveds!' her voice wailed down to them.

'Not lost long enough, Wilhelmina,' muttered Mr Majeika. Then he turned to the Worshipful Wizard. 'Goodbye, sir, and goodbye, Aunty, and goodbye, all of you – and thanks for the best Barty Party ever!'

* * *

'Goodbye, everyone,' Mr Majeika was saying to Mr Potter, Mrs Brace-Girdle and all the others in School Cottage. 'Thank you for the most magical party ever – I've had such a wonderful time and it's been quite exhausting!'

'You can't go yet, Majeika,' said Mr Potter. 'Here's your birthday cake. And of course you've got to blow out all the candles!'

Mr Majeika took a great gasp of air. But all that running to and fro from the Bluebell Wood finally took its toll of him. As he puffed at the candles – blowing them all out – he collapsed in a heap, right on top of Mrs Brace-Girdle's cake.

Thomas and Melanie looked at each other and grinned.

'Birthdays can be very tiring occasions,' said Melanie.

'What a good thing,' said Thomas, 'that he only has them once every forty-seven years.'

4

GHOSTCLUSTERS

So Mr Majeika's birthday was kept after all – but Walpurgis Night! That was a different matter.

Poor Mr Majeika. It was his first Walpurgis Night away from Walpurgis and he knew he would have to celebrate it all by himself. Walpurgis Night was the biggest night of the year, up there in the land in the sky where the Wizards and the Witches come from, and every Walpurgian always tried to be back home that night, so that they wouldn't miss the marvellous celebrations – the dancing around the Everlasting Bonfire, the Marrowbone and Bromide Supper, and most of all the unforgettable sight of the Witches' Knitting Circle performing the Dance of the Seven Cobwebs. But poor Mr Majeika! There was no way that *he* could get back to Walpurgis for this year's festivities. He had been banished to Britland, and there he must stay, as a teacher, until he had proved himself worthy to return home and complete his Sorcery Exams.

'Poor Majeika!' mused the Worshipful Wizard,

as he contemplated the plight of the little chap down there in Britland. 'Poor Majeika! Walpurgis Night, and he'll be all by himself.'

'Poor me,' Mr Majeika was thinking, down there at his windmill. 'Walpurgis Night and I'll be all by myself.' But he had decided to organize his own Walpurgis celebrations, and pretend he was back in Walpurgis with all the other Wizards and Witches. He had built an enormous bonfire, piling it high with oddly named wild flowers and strange weeds from the hedgerows, and he had made himself a crown of bogweed, just like everyone would be wearing up there in Walpurgis. That night, when he got back from school, he would light it and dance round it in the moonlight, chanting Walpurgian chants.

He couldn't wait!

'Ah, Majeika,' said Mr Potter, when Mr Majeika rolled up at St Barty's School that morning on his trike, 'it's a very special day today, isn't it?'

'Yes, yes, Mr Potter,' said Mr Majeika eagerly, 'but how did you know?' For a moment, he wondered whether Walpurgis Night was celebrated in Much Barty. How exciting that would be! He could imagine Mrs Brace-Girdle and the village ladies dancing round a bonfire; they'd look almost as remarkable as the Witches' Knitting Circle.

'How did I know, Majeika?' asked Mr Potter, puzzled. 'Why, because I organized the whole thing myself.'

'Organized it, Mr Potter?'

'Yes, yes, Majeika – the annual School Outing. You haven't forgotten, Majeika, have you? We're going on our annual school trip and this year the destination is Chutney Castle.'

'Really, Mr Potter?' said Mr Majeika. 'That sounds exciting.' Not quite as exciting as Walpurgis Night, perhaps, but still pretty good. He had never seen a Britland castle, though he had visited several in distant parts of Walpurgis, most of them occupied by rather dangerous giants and ogres.

'Chutney Castle,' said Mr Potter impressively, 'has been standing, Majeika, since the tenth century.'

'Has it really!' said Mr Majeika. 'Wouldn't it rather sit down?'

'Poor Majeika,' said the Worshipful Wizard yet again. And this time he was saying it out loud to one of the Senior Wizards, Wizard Thymes. 'If there was only some way we could keep him in touch with our Walpurgis Night celebrations up here . . .'

Wizard Thymes scratched his head with the end of his wand. 'Hmm,' he said thoughtfully. 'Perhaps if one of us were to go down and visit him?'

The Worshipful Wizard gave a shudder. 'Well, not one of *us*,' he said firmly. 'I've been already, and it was awful.' He was remembering the thorn bushes, and all the wind on the way down.

'Possibly,' said Wizard Thymes, 'some junior

Walpurgian, someone who would be willing to get a little fresh air and see the wide world?'

A big coach was parked outside St Barty's School, with the words *Jolly Jasper's Merrie Medieval Tours* painted on the side. 'All set, everyone?' called Mr Potter. 'The bus will take us to the station, where as a special treat we shall be going by steam train to Chutney Junction, where another bus will pick us up and deliver us to Chutney Castle. All aboard, everyone!'

'Can't go yet,' said the driver. 'Jolly Jasper, the boss, hasn't turned up.'

'But it's already ten o'clock,' said Mr Potter anxiously. 'At this rate the children will miss the delicious lunch that has been arranged for them at Chutney Castle.'

'I'll tell you what,' said Councillor Mrs Brace-Girdle, who had come to see her daughter Melanie off, 'I'll wait here for this Jolly Jasper person and bring him on by car. No reason why he should spoil your day.'

'That's very good of you, Bunty,' said Mr Potter. 'Mrs Brace-Girdle to the rescue, as usual. Off we go, everyone! Next stop, the station.'

'Station?' asked Mr Majeika. 'What's a station?'

The Worshipful Wizard had called a meeting of all the Walpurgians. He made a little speech about how lonely Majeika would be. 'So,' he concluded, 'who would like to pop down there, just for a day and a night, and make Apprentice Wizard Majeika a really happy Walpurgian, by celebrating Walpurgis Night with him?'

No one put their hand up. (Wilhelmina Worlock had gone on a day trip to the back of the moon and so was not there to volunteer.)

'Hm,' said the Worshipful Wizard. 'I see, no volunteers.' He turned to Wizard Thymes. 'That makes things a little difficult.'

Wizard Thymes scratched his head once again. 'Well,' he said, 'not everyone is here, you know. There is one name I can think of. And he just *might* agree to go. If you want to see him, we'll have to go down to the Catacombs . . .'

'Well,' said Melanie to Mr Majeika, 'now you know what a station looks like.' They were standing on the platform, waiting for the special steam train.

'Yes,' said Mr Majeika doubtfully, looking around him. 'But I still don't know what it's for.'

'I'll explain,' said Thomas. 'You see – '

But at that moment there was a shriek of a whistle, and they could see the steam train puffing towards them down the line.

Mr Majeika screamed in fright and took to his heels. 'A dragon! It's a dragon!'

Thomas and Melanie ran after him and caught hold of him, dragging him back out of the waiting room, where he was trying to hide. 'It isn't a dragon,' said Melanie firmly. 'It's just a train.'

The train pulled in, and the engine steamed past them, with its fire roaring in the cab. Mr Majeika was shaking all over with fright. 'Look! Fire, fire!

And steam and smoke!' he cried. 'Only dragons breathe steam and smoke and have fires in their bellies like that.'

'Ah, there you are, Majeika,' said Mr Potter, strolling down the platform. 'In you get.'

'I'm not riding on a dragon, Mr Potter,' quivered Mr Majeika.

'Oh yes you are,' said Melanie firmly. 'All aboard, Mr Majeika!'

The Walpurgian Catacombs are the darkest, ghostliest and ghastliest place in all Walpurgis, hung with cobwebs and lit with a sinister greenish light. Even the Worshipful Wizard was a little nervous as he and Wizard Thymes groped their way down a narrow passage.

'Are you sure this is the right place, Thymes?' asked the Worshipful Wizard anxiously. 'I wouldn't want to take a wrong turning – you never know what you might meet.'

'No indeed,' said Wizard Thymes. 'But this should be the right chamber. If I remember, he lives in a glass coffin in here.' He ducked under a narrow archway and led the Worshipful Wizard into a particularly eerie-looking cave.

'A glass coffin?' asked the Worshipful Wizard. 'Did you say coffin?'

'Well, well, isn't this exciting, children?' said Mr Potter, surveying the chaos around him in the train.

Fighting had broken out among Class Three the

moment the whistle had blown and the train set off from Much Barty. Several of them had got into the luggage rack and the rest of them were quarrelling about who could have seats next to the windows.

'Ah, Majeika,' said Mr Potter, seeing Mr Majeika tottering nervously down the corridor, 'you can take charge.' And Mr Potter went and shut himself in the toilet.

'T–take ch–charge, Mr Potter?' said Mr Majeika nervously, peering out of the corridor window. 'J–just as you say. But shouldn't someone keep an eye on that dragon? It's still breathing fire, you know.'

Thomas and Melanie, looking for seats, found an empty compartment. Empty, that is, save for Hamish Bigmore, who was sitting there all by himself, sprinkling salt on to a bag of crisps.

'Mind if we join you, Hamish?' asked Melanie.

'Most certainly I mind,' said Hamish Bigmore. 'I've got my dad's season ticket, and he always travels First Class. Get out, before I call the guard!' And he pointed at the *First Class Ticket Holders Only* sign on the window.

Wizard Thymes had found the glass coffin, and was knocking on it. 'Come out, come out, whoever you are!' he intoned.

The glass was dirty, and the Worshipful Wizard couldn't see who, or what, was inside the coffin. 'Are you sure this is a good idea?' he asked anxiously.

110

'It's the proper spell to raise them, you know,' said Wizard Thymes. And he intoned again: 'Come out, come out, whoever you are!'

The glass coffin began to creak open.

Mr Majeika was beginning to get used to the fact that they were travelling by dragon. After all, the dreadful creature hadn't eaten them yet. But he could imagine what it would be like if it did. A big mouth would open and suddenly everything would go dark as you were popped into the dragon's tummy.

At that moment everything went dark.

Mr Majeika screamed.

'It's all right, Mr Majeika!' called Melanie.

'The dragon's swallowed us up!' yelled Mr Majeika.

'No it hasn't,' said Thomas soothingly. 'We're just in a tunnel, that's all.'

Mr Potter emerged from the toilet. 'Ah, Majeika,' he said, 'you look as if you're enjoying yourself. Nothing like a nice relaxing day out, is there?'

'No, Mr Potter,' quivered Mr Majeika.

'Come out, come out, whoever you are!' intoned Wizard Thymes yet again, and lit up the end of his wand so that the greenish light in the cave became a little stronger.

'Go away,' said a little voice from the crack where the coffin had opened. 'I don't like the light. It makes me nervous.'

'Come out, come out, whoever you are!' repeated Wizard Thymes.

'Shan't,' said the little voice.

'Oh, yes, you will,' said Wizard Thymes firmly, putting his hand in the crack. 'Out you come!'

And out, very unwillingly, came a thin shivering little ghost with long grey hair and a face as white as a sheet.

'This,' said Wizard Thymes to the Worshipful Wizard, 'is Phil Spectre.'

The pale little face stared up at them.

'Phil Spectre,' announced the Worshipful Wizard, 'you have been chosen to visit Britland.'

'Please, no!' shivered the ghost, trying to get back into the glass coffin. But Wizard Thymes got hold of him by the neck.

'It's an order,' he told the ghost.

'No!' shrieked the ghost, wriggling so hard that his head fell off. 'It always does that when I'm frightened,' he explained, putting it on again.

'Listen, Spectre,' said the Worshipful Wizard firmly, 'you can't spend the rest of your life – I mean death – hanging about in this miserable coffin. Get out and do the job for which you were trained! You're supposed to haunt people.'

'That's right, Spectre,' said Wizard Thymes. 'It's high time you spooked.'

'But I don't want to haunt anyone, sir,' said Phil Spectre miserably. 'I'm too – too shy. I used to do a bit of haunting, on the quiet, but I kept scaring myself to death. That's why I hide away here, sir, with nothing but a few other ghosts flitting past now and then.'

'You are a wretched little fellow, aren't you?' observed the Worshipful Wizard. 'Don't you ever get lonely?'

'Well, sir,' said Phil Spectre, 'a bit, now and then.'

'Exactly so. Well, Apprentice Wizard Majeika is *very* lonely, down there in Britland, and you have been chosen to go and cheer him up – just for the one night, Walpurgis Night.'

'But, sir – '

'I won't hear another word against it, Spectre. Off you go!' But he wouldn't. So Wizard Thymes and the Worshipful Wizard had to push poor Phil Spectre through the hole that leads from Walpurgis into the sky, and down to Britland. The poor creature screamed as he fell.

If he had been wearing a white sheet, such as ghosts often put on, it would have acted as a parachute. But he was a medieval-style ghost, since he dated from the days of Henry the Eighth, and his doublet and hose didn't act as any kind of brake against the wind. He fell very fast and landed with a bump in a field just outside Much Barty. Ghosts weigh nothing at all, so he was not hurt, but the whole thing had been a frightful shock.

'Moo!' said a cow just behind him and poor Phil Spectre would have leapt out of his skin, if he had had a skin. As it was, he gave a little scream, and the book of *Instructions for Walpurgians in the Country of the Britlanders* fell out of his pocket.

That reminded him. He was supposed to look up his orders in the book. 'Upon arrival in Much Barty,' he read, 'make yourself known immediately to Apprentice Wizard Majeika, who will usually be found at St Barty's School.'

Phil Spectre set off down the road.

'Right,' muttered Mrs Brace-Girdle, getting into her car and slamming the door. 'I'm off. Drat this Jolly Jasper character for not turning up and keeping me waiting for no purpose. I'm off!'

She had just put the car into gear when she saw someone in medieval costume walking down the road.

'So there you are!' snorted Mrs Brace-Girdle, winding down her window. 'A fine time to arrive, I must say. Hop in the back. The door isn't locked.'

So it wasn't, but Phil Spectre didn't need to open doors. He passed through this one and materialized on the other side, sitting himself down on the back seat of Mrs Brace-Girdle's car. There was nothing about this Britlander in his handbook, but he recognized in Mrs Brace-Girdle the look of someone who expects to be obeyed.

'Now,' said Mrs Brace-Girdle, driving off, 'we'll have you at Chutney Castle in no time.'

At Chutney Castle, the owner, Lord Reg Pickles, stared gloomily out of the window at the St Barty's School party, which was just getting out of the coach. 'Not another bloomin' school party,' muttered Lord Reg.

'Never mind, dearie,' said his wife, Lady Lillie. 'Helps to pay the bills, don't it, Reg?'

Outside, Mr Potter was explaining the history of Chutney Castle to Mr Majeika. 'The present owner is Lord Reg Pickles, the founder of Bartyshire's famous Plumptious Pickled Onions and Gourmet Gherkins, delicacies which no doubt you have often sampled, Majeika?'

'Not me, Mr Potter,' said Mr Majeika.

'And here he is, children,' called Mr Potter, seeing Lord Reg emerging from under the entrance arch. 'An actual member of the Great British Aristocracy! A real live Lord!'

'Pleased to meet you, children,' said Lord Reg, who was clutching a jar of Plumptious Pickled Onions. 'May I present my wife, the Lady Lillie?'

'All right, you lot,' called Lady Lillie. 'The Souvenir Shop is over there. Get your money out!'

The children made a stampede for souvenirs. 'My, isn't this fun, Majeika?' said Mr Potter. 'A real piece of history.'

'Yes, Mr Potter,' said Mr Majeika dutifully.

'Oh, and Majeika, would you supervise the unloading of the overnight bags?'

'Bags, Mr Potter? What sort of bags?'

'Suitcases, my dear chap. Don't say you didn't bring one? Surely you knew we were going to stay the night?'

'No, I didn't,' said Mr Majeika miserably,

thinking of his Walpurgis Night bonfire, which now he would never have the chance to light.

Mrs Brace-Girdle, who was still very cross, was driving rather fast. She came round a corner and, finding that there was a red traffic light in front of her, had to brake hard. The car bumped to a halt and Phil Spectre's head fell off.

There was a policeman on duty by the traffic lights, and Mrs Brace-Girdle rolled down her window. 'Constable, can you tell me the way to Chutney Castle?'

The policeman came over and told her. The lights changed to green, and as the car drove off the policeman turned rather green too. There had been a person on the back seat holding his head on his lap. And the head had turned and looked at him.

Lady Lillie Pickles was taking – or rather, dragging – the children on a conducted tour of the castle. In particular, she was dragging Hamish Bigmore, who had ignored every sign that said 'Do Not Touch'.

'This way, children,' she called. 'And remember, don't touch a thing.'

While her back was turned, Hamish picked up an antique vase labelled 'Chinese, Ming Period'.

'My dad's got nicer stuff than that,' said Hamish.

Lady Lillie turned and saw the vase in his hand. 'I said *don't touch*!' she snapped and smacked his hand.

Then one of the other children tripped over a rope and her attention was distracted. Hamish dropped the vase and it shattered into a million pieces.

'Oh, no!' breathed Thomas.

But Mr Majeika was bringing up the rear of the file of children and he caught sight of the disaster. In a moment he had flicked his tuft of hair and – magically – the vase had reassembled itself and floated up to the place on the table where it had been sitting.

Only Thomas and Melanie spotted this. They looked at each other.

'He's still – ' said Melanie.

' – magical, Melanie,' said Thomas.

'Magnificent, isn't it, Majeika?' said Mr Potter to Mr Majeika as they entered the Great Hall.

'Very nice, Mr Potter,' said Mr Majeika. 'But I used to live in a huge place just like this, you know.'

'You never?' said Lord Reg, impressed. 'What, you mean with a load of proper lords and ladies and all that?'

'No,' said Mr Majeika, 'with a load of proper Wizards and Witches. I mean – it was a very wizard place.'

'Oh yeah?' said Lord Reg. 'Course, we weren't a Lord and Lady from birth, you know.'

'Really?' said Mr Potter. 'You do surprise me, your lordship.'

'Nope,' said Lord Reg. 'The missus, when I first knew her, was an onion pickler in Poplar.'

'You don't say,' remarked Mr Potter. 'I'd never have guessed, would you, Majeika?'

'Certainly not, Mr Potter,' said Mr Majeika.

'Course, we're full of class now,' said Lord Reg. 'Yes, it's surprising what pickled onions can do for a man, Mr Potter.' He gave a loud burp.

'Yes?' said Mr Potter politely.

'Yup,' said Lord Reg, patting his stomach. 'I mean, once yer onions takes off, you can be a real big noise.' He burped again.

'I must say,' said Mrs Brace-Girdle, turning down the lane that was signposted *To Chutney Castle*, 'for someone who calls himself Jolly Jasper, you are remarkably silent.'

On the back seat, Phil Spectre was fitting his head on to his shoulders again. He made no reply.

'And you can leave *that* alone too,' snapped Lady Lillie, snatching Hamish Bigmore away from a medieval instrument of torture, into which he had been trying to squeeze the foot of a small boy from Class Three.

' Well, your lordship,' observed Mr Potter, looking around the dungeon, 'you've certainly got everything here.'

'Nearly everything, Mr Potter,' answered Lord Reg, opening his jar and offering Mr Potter a pickled onion. 'There is just one thing what we lack, what would be the icing on the pickle, so to speak, if we had it.'

'And what's that, Lord Pickles?' asked Mr Majeika.

'A resident Ghost,' said Lord Reg Pickles, popping an onion into his mouth.

Mrs Brace-Girdle parked her car by the castle drawbridge and got out, banging her door shut. 'You'd better wait in there till I've told them that Jolly Jasper has arrived,' she said. 'It might be quite the wrong moment if you rushed in there now.'

She strode under the archway, up the main staircase and into the Great Hall. Lord Reg was just leading Mr Potter and Mr Majeika back from the dungeons.

'Ah, Mr Potter!' said Mrs Brace-Girdle. 'I've brought him with me. Is it all right for me to send him in straight away?'

'Who, Bunty?' asked Mr Potter, puzzled.

'Why,' said Mrs Brace-Girdle, 'Jolly Jasper, the Merrie Minstrel.'

'Jolly Jasper?' repeated Mr Potter, puzzled. 'But Jolly Jasper has been here for hours. He met us at Chutney Junction and drove the coach up here. He's down in the courtyard right now, playing his lute.'

Mrs Brace-Girdle's face fell. 'Then who have I brought in my car?'

* * *

Downstairs, by the drawbridge, Lady Lillie was looking after the combined Souvenir Shop and ticket office. She heard the turnstile creak; someone must be arriving.

'Yes?' she said. 'Adult ticket? Child or old age pensioner?'

Phil Spectre, who was rather short, picked his head off his shoulders with one hand and held it up to the ticket window.

'Ghost ticket, please,' said the head.

Lady Lillie screamed.

'Now, children!' called Mr Potter. 'It's time to go and look at the suits of armour in the Long Gallery. This is a particularly dark and sinister part of the castle, so don't forget to watch out for any ghosts!' He turned to Mr Majeika. 'Just my little joke, Majeika. I don't believe in ghosts.'

'Don't you, Mr Potter?' said Mr Majeika nervously. He knew all about ghosts from Walpurgis. They were sinister fellows who lived down in the Catacombs, where most Witches and Wizards didn't like to go at all. He'd never seen one and he didn't want to start now.

'Don't worry, Mr Majeika,' said Melanie, who could see he was nervous. 'We'll protect you from the ghosts.'

'Ghosts!' snorted Hamish Bigmore. 'Only babies believe in ghosts!'

Phil Spectre thought the castle looked rather nice inside – just the place to do a haunting, if you were that way inclined – but he was frightfully nervous. He kept hearing distant voices, as if there were . . . *people* about.

Some ghosts don't believe in people but Phil Spectre knew better. Down there in the Catacombs of Walpurgis, his granny ghost had told him horrifying tales about people who came in the night to frighten poor little ghosts; people who opened doors, rather than gliding through the woodwork; people who walked up and downstairs, rather than floating in the air; people who spoke words, rather than giving moans and shrieks; people who had horrible things like cameras and tape-recorders and radios, rather than a nice comforting iron ball and chain; people who were made of flesh and blood, rather than being just a wisp of ecto-plasm, or a bone-rattling skeleton. 'But it's all right, my poor little ghostie,' she had told him. 'If you're lucky, you may never meet a – person!'

Now, in Chutney Castle, poor Phil Spectre knew he was *surrounded* by people. He looked for somewhere to hide.

He found a room full of suits of armour. One of those would do nicely.

'Here we are, then, children,' said Mr Potter, as they came into the armoury. 'Most of this armour dates from the days of Henry the Eighth. Isn't it magnificent?'

'Load of rusty old rubbish,' said Hamish Big-more. 'They'd have done better to melt it all down

121

into baked bean cans. Yah!' And he took hold of the biggest suit of armour and shook it so that it rattled noisily.

Inside, poor Phil Spectre was being shaken about dreadfully. His granny was right! People were awful. He was terrified. And he was also very angry. What right had this creature to come and frighten him like that? He'd show it!

Hamish Bigmore turned his back on the suit of armour. 'Baked beans,' he sneered. 'I'd rather have a can of baked beans. *Oucchh*!'

The suit of armour had kicked him very hard on the bottom.

Thomas and Melanie had seen it happen and were laughing till tears ran down their faces. 'It must have been a ghost, Hamish!' said Thomas.

Hamish Bigmore scowled at them. 'It just tipped over and kicked me by accident,' he said. 'Only babies believe in ghosts.'

'W–was it really a ghost?' Mr Majeika asked Thomas and Melanie, when they were back in the Great Hall.

'Search us,' said Thomas. 'But there was something in there that kicked Hamish.'

'And it certainly wasn't us,' said Melanie. 'I wouldn't be in the least surprised if, in an old castle like this, there wasn't a ghost floating about the place.'

'Oh d–dear,' said Mr Majeika.

* * *

Phil Spectre had some difficulty in getting out of the suit of armour. He wondered where it was really safe to hide. Then he remembered that he shouldn't be hiding at all. He should be looking for Mr Majeika. How had he got carried off to this wretched castle? He was supposed to be in Much Barty, searching for Mr Majeika at the school.

Suddenly he heard a voice in the passage outside. He froze; it was a *person* again – how frightening!

'Mr Majeika!' called the voice (it was Thomas). 'Mr Majeika! The rooms we're going to sleep in are upstairs. Are you coming up to see your bedroom?'

Phil Spectre couldn't believe his ears. Mr Majeika was here – in the castle! What a stroke of luck. Now all he had to do was to find him and introduce himself to this fellow Walpurgian. But if only he could manage it without running into any more *people*.

Very cautiously, he stuck his head through the door and peeped out. Yes, the coast seemed to be clear. Silently, he floated out and up the stairs towards the bedrooms.

In his bedroom, Mr Majeika gave a flick of his tuft of hair, and there stood an overnight bag containing night-shirt, toothbrush and night-cap. 'There,' he said, 'that should do it.'

'Gosh,' said Thomas.

'Well,' said Melanie, 'sleep well, Mr Majeika.

I'm sure there aren't any ghosts here really, and if there are, they probably won't disturb you.'

'I hope n–not,' said Mr Majeika.

Outside, Phil Spectre was groping his way nervously along the dark corridor. Which door should he try?

Lady Lillie Pickles was taking her teeth out for the night when she heard her bedroom door open behind her. 'Is that you, Reg?' she asked without looking round. 'Make us a mug of cocoa, there's a dear. All those Gourmet Gherkins we had for supper have given me a touch of wind.'

There was no reply. Lady Lillie looked in her mirror – and saw a ghostly pale head regarding her from the doorway. She screamed.

When he had got back his nerve – the encounter with the lady who could take out her teeth (something no ghost had ever learnt to do) had thoroughly frightened him – Phil Spectre floated on down the corridor. 'Mr Majeika!' he called softly, in case the Apprentice Wizard could somehow hear him. 'Mr Majeika!'

Mr Majeika was just dropping off to sleep when he thought he heard someone calling his name. Was it Thomas or Melanie? Yawning, he got out of bed and tiptoed to the door. The whole place still frightened him. Why did they have to come to this horrible creepy castle, especially on Walpurgis Night, when he wanted to be at home, dancing round his bonfire?

He opened the door. There was no one in the corridor.

But again he heard the voice. 'Mr Majeika!' it called softly.

Shivering with cold and nerves, Mr Majeika gingerly walked to where he thought the voice came from.

'Mr Majeika!' called Phil Spectre desperately. His nerves were getting quite worn down. If he didn't find the Apprentice Wizard soon, he'd get on to Walpurgis and demand that they take him back at once. He might even get back in time for some of the famous Walpurgis Night celebrations he had heard so much about, but had never yet attended.

There was nobody to be seen and the place was utterly silent. Yes, surely they would let him go home now.

He turned a corner – and ran smack into Mr Majeika! He screamed and his head fell off.

Mr Majeika yelled out – and yelled again when he saw the head bouncing along the floor.

Phil's body ran one way and his head bounced the other way.

Mr Majeika turned and ran but he couldn't find the way back to his room. He kept taking wrong turnings in the dark and it was a full ten minutes before he had groped his way back to his own room.

Meanwhile Phil had managed to find his head. Without stopping to put it on, he rushed for safety – into the nearest open door he could find.

And this open door just happened (though he didn't know it) to be the door to Mr Majeika's bedroom.

'Phew! my room at last,' murmured Mr Majeika, sinking wearily on to the bed and pulling back the bedclothes so that he could collapse into bed.

From the bed, Phil Spectre's head stared up, terrified, at Mr Majeika.

Thomas and Melanie heard the shrieks and hurried into Mr Majeika's room in their night things, blinking the sleep out of their eyes. 'There *is* a ghost!' gasped Mr Majeika, pointing a shaking hand at Phil.

'Yes,' said Thomas. 'So we can see. And surely ghosts are Walpurgians aren't they?' Mr Majeika nodded. 'So,' went on Thomas, 'why don't you two say hello to each other in the proper way?'

Phil Spectre stared at Thomas, then at Mr Majeika and then he began to smile. 'Apprentice Wizard Majeika?' he said nervously.

Mr Majeika, who had begun to smile too, nodded. 'Apprentice Spook – ?'

'Spectre, sir,' said Phil Spectre; and he and Mr Majeika pulled each other's noses, which is how all proper Walpurgians always greet each other.

'But what in the name of Walpurgis are you doing down here, and on Walpurgis Night too?' asked Mr Majeika.

'It was all the Worshipful Wizard's idea,'

explained Phil Spectre. '"Off you go," he said, "and cheer up Majeika."'

'Did he?' asked Mr Majeika excitedly. 'Did he really?'

'Just so you wouldn't be alone on Walpurgis Night.'

'Well, well,' said Mr Majeika. And then a thought crossed his mind. 'Apprentice Spook Spectre, you wouldn't like a job, would you?'

'A job, Apprentice Wizard Majeika?' asked Phil Spectre nervously.

'A haunting,' explained Mr Majeika. 'A real permanent haunting. A lovely historical castle, all to yourself. And lots of real people to frighten?'

'A castle? People?' said Phil Spectre anxiously. 'Oh, no – no, not yet. I'm too young.'

'How old are you?' asked Thomas.

'Four hundred and thirty,' said Phil Spectre.

'Well, then,' said Mr Majeika, 'I should have thought you were just about old enough for a real haunting job. Right here, in Chutney Castle.'

Lord Reg and Lady Lillie were rather surprised to be woken in the middle of the night, especially when Mr Majeika explained that he wanted to introduce them to a ghost. But when Lady Lillie had got over her fright, she began to take to Phil.

'Oh, isn't he a little love, Reg?' she cooed.

'He certainly is, my little Pickalillie,' said Lord Reg. 'Just think of all the lovely visitors he'll bring us. The Ghost of Chutney Castle! We can advertise him on all the posters.'

'But I'm a shy ghost,' said Phil nervously to Mr Majeika. 'Tell 'em I'm shy.'

'*I* was shy when I started work as a teacher, Phil,' said Mr Majeika. 'But this Britland life does wonders for you. You'll love it.'

Phil thought for a moment. 'Can I sleep in a turret?' he asked hopefully.

'Of course,' said Lord Reg.

'A really smelly old turret, where no *people* would dare to go?'

'The West Tower is full of mouldy onions that didn't take to pickling,' said Lady Lillie. 'No one ever sets foot there.'

'Oh, Mr Majeika,' said Phil Spectre, smiling. 'Just think of it, a real turret of my own. Why, I can gibber in the moonlight and go flying out among the bats. I just can't wait!'

'Seems Phil Spectre isn't coming back,' said the Worshipful Wizard. 'Majeika has applied for a permanent absence for him. He's got a real haunting job.'

'Splendid,' said Wizard Thymes. 'We ought to mark that on Majeika's Progress chart. He's doing really well this term.'

'And apparently he and Phil Spectre had a jolly Walpurgis Night together, eating – what was it he said? – pickled onions.'

'Ugh!' said Wizard Thymes. 'No accounting for Britland taste. Give me a bogweed sandwich any day.'

5

GONNA WASH THOSE SPELLS RIGHT OUT OF MY HAIR

'La, la, la,' trilled Mr Majeika, singing a merry Walpurgis melody as he poured ditchwater from a bucket into the big bowl in which he washed his face and hands. 'La, la, la.' Mr Majeika was at his windmill and it was a bright sunny morning. He had just got up and had breakfast and now he was going to wash his hair.

Wizards don't wash their hair as often as you do. Maybe you only wash your hair about once a year when somebody makes you do it, although you ought to wash it at least once a week. Wizards only wash their hair every sixty-second year. Even less often, in other words, than they have birthdays.

You may already have guessed the reason. A wizard's hair isn't just hair. Certainly not for Mr Majeika. As you know, Mr Majeika had a very special use for his hair, or at least for a certain bit of it. He wiggled the tuft in the middle, at the top of his head, to make spells. And when you've just washed your hair, you can't wiggle it, however hard you try. It's all soft and silky, which is very nice if you are going out to a party, but not much good if you want to do a spell. So that's why wizards don't get through much shampoo. Even quite a small bottle will last them a thousand years.

'La, la, la,' sang Mr Majeika, splashing ditch-water over his head, and scrubbing away with Hecate Hair Preparation, the Shampoo for Wizards with Mild Dandruff. 'La, la, la.' Washing it was always a risk. You waited sixty-two years and then, of course, you chose a day when it turned out (*after* you'd washed your hair) that you did need to do a spell after all. Which could be very awkward. But Mr Majeika was sure that this wouldn't happen today. After all, it was a nice sunny day in Much Barty and all was right with the world. Why on earth should he need to do any magic?

'Ah, Majeika, glorious weather, isn't it?' said Mr Potter when Mr Majeika arrived at school. 'Just the perfect day for it.'

'The perfect day for what, Mr Potter?' asked Mr Majeika. Scarcely a day seemed to go by in Much Barty without something special happening – a Fête, or a School Trip, or a ceremony. Mr Potter always seemed to have something new up his sleeve. Really, thought Mr Majeika, these Britlanders do lead an exhausting life. 'What is it today, Mr Potter?' he asked rather anxiously.

'Don't you remember?' said Mr Potter. 'The Village Show. Isn't that exciting, Majeika?'

130

'Yes,' said Mr Majeika, 'it certainly is. But – could you remind me, Mr Potter, what do we, er, *do* at a Village Show?'

'Do, Majeika? Why, we have stalls.'

'Stalls, Mr Potter? Do you mean things that horses are kept in?'

'No, no, different kinds of stalls, selling things – produce, handicrafts, flans, home made marmalade, all that kind of thing. And then – and this is the really exciting bit – we *show* things, Majeika.'

'Show them, Mr Potter? You mean, films and that sort of thing?'

'No, Majeika. I mean flowers and vegetables. My own specialization, Majeika, is zucchinis. I'm renowned throughout Bartyshire for my giant zucchinis.'

'Zooky-knees, Mr Potter?' said Mr Majeika. 'Isn't that a kind of muscial instrument? I used to play something like that in our band back in Walpurgis – I mean, back home.'

'A zucchini isn't a musical instrument, Majeika,' said Mr Potter disapprovingly. 'It's a kind of courgette.'

'A quartet, Mr Potter? You mean like a string quartet?'

'No, no,' said Mr Potter impatiently. 'Look, Majeika, I'll show you one.' He leant over the wall of School Cottage and picked up a large green marrow about two feet long. 'There you are,' he said proudly. 'That's bound to be this year's prizewinner.'

'Very nice,' said Mr Majeika dutifully. 'But what

131

do you do with it, Mr Potter? Do you hit someone over the head with it?'

'Good heavens no. The judges come and measure it.'

'Measure it, Mr Potter? Whatever for?'

'Why, Majeika, to see who has grown the biggest one.'

Mr Majeika sighed. 'And Britlanders really like doing this?' he asked. The place would never cease to puzzle him.

Outside the village hall, where the Show was to take place, Councillor Mrs Bunty Brace-Girdle was, as usual, issuing orders.

'Now,' she said, reading out to her helpers from a list, 'Wooden toys will be manned by Mr Blizzard. The raffia stall will be looked after by Miss Gosling, if she can find her reading glasses. Any volunteers for stuffed savouries? Well, we'll get someone. And Mr Potter,' she called, catching sight of the headmaster, 'I though you might like to take charge of the jumble.'

'Ah, yes, Bunty, I anticipated that,' said Mr Potter smoothly. He wasn't going to let anyone, not even Mrs Brace-Girdle, take him away from his giant zucchini. 'I have passed on the job to Mr Majeika here.'

'Have you, Mr Potter?' asked Mr Majeika, utterly flummoxed by this sudden news.

'Have you!' snorted Mrs Brace-Girdle angrily. 'I really don't think that Mr Majeika will be able to – '

132

'Oh yes he will,' cut in Mr Potter. 'Mr Majeika knows all about jumble, don't you, Majeika?'

'All about – what?' asked Mr Majeika desperately.

'*Jumble*,' said Mr Potter firmly. 'Spelt J-U-M-B-L-E.'

'J-U-M-B-L-E,' said Mr Majeika to himself, 'That spells *Jumbly*, doesn't it? Very well, Mr Potter, I'll look after the Jumbly. How do you look after it, Mr Potter? Does it need feeding? Is it fierce? Can you take it out for walks?'

'We'll explain it to you,' said Melanie, after she and Thomas had found Mr Majeika sitting forlornly on the steps of the village hall, muttering 'Jumbly? What is a Jumbly?' to himself.

'You see,' said Thomas, 'it's – well, sort of old stuff.'

'Broken stuff,' said Melanie.

'You know, things no one wants,' said Thomas.

'Or wants any more,' added Melanie. 'Maybe they did once, but now they've grown out of them.'

'Or just don't need them,' said Thomas. 'Understand?'

Mr Majeika nodded. 'I think so,' he said. 'Any old stuff that's lying about and people aren't using it.'

'That's it,' said Thomas.

'Well,' said Melanie, 'just about.'

'Now, Mr Majeika,' said Mrs Brace-Girdle, bustling up to him half an hour before the Village Show was due to begin, 'everything ready?'

'Oh, yes, Mrs Brace-Girdle,' said Mr Majeika, showing her his smart stall, over which Thomas and Melanie had draped a sign saying 'JUMBLE: EVERYTHING GOING CHEAP.'

'That's the ticket,' said Mrs Brace-Girdle. 'But where's your stuff?' she added, surveying the stall, which was entirely empty.

'My stuff?' asked Mr Majeika, puzzled.

'The jumble. Got it all ready in boxes, have you?'

Mr Majeika shook his head. 'I was waiting for them to bring it,' he said. 'They do bring it, don't they?'

Mrs Brace-Girdle frowned. 'Bring it, Mr Majeika? What do you mean?'

'I thought people brought the Jumbly to me, and all I had to do was measure it, and tell them who'd got the biggest one.'

'The biggest what, Mr Majeika?' asked Mrs Brace-Girdle icily.

'The biggest – what was it called again? – zooky-knees,' said Mr Majeika.

'Mummy's very cross,' Melanie told Mr Majeika. 'She thought you were pulling her leg.'

'Pulling her leg?' said Mr Majeika, astonished. 'Why, I never touched her.'

'She said you were talking some nonsense about measuring people's knees. She said I was to tell you to get some jumble, and get it fast, or she'd complain about you to Mr Potter. And you know she's a governor of the school, don't you?'

'Yes,' said Mr Majeika gloomily. 'So I'm sup-posed to find the Jumbly myself, am I, and then measure it?'

'I don't know where you got this measuring idea, Mr Majeika,' said Thomas. 'Just find some jumble, somewhere or other, and with a bit of luck people will buy it.'

'Very well,' said Mr Majeika crestfallen. 'Now, what was it you said Jumbly is? Any old stuff that's lying about and no one is using . . .' and off he went.

Mr Majeika knocked on the door of School Cottage but there was no reply. 'Mr Potter must have gone to the village hall with his zooky-knees,' he said to himself. 'Well, he always leaves the door unlocked.' He pushed it open and went in.

In the hall, the grandfather clock struck a quarter past. 'Oh dear, I must hurry,' said Mr Majeika. 'Now I was going to ask Mr Potter to tell me where to get the Jumbly. Now I'll have to find it for myself. Let me think: "Any old stuff that's lying about and no one is using."' He stared around him. And his eye was caught by the grandfather clock.

'Well,' he said to himself, 'nobody's using *that* for a start. I've seen Mr Potter walk past it a hundred times and never even give it a glance. Bong, bong, bong, every quarter of an hour – it'd drive me mad! I bet he'll be only too glad to get rid of it.'

* * *

Mr Potter was setting out his carrots, onions and giant zucchini on the competitors' stall in the Produce section when he heard a jangly noise. Mr Majeika was staggering into the village hall behind an enormous grandfather clock.

'Good gracious,' said Mr Potter, peering over his glasses 'What have you got there, Majeika?'

'Something – for – the – Jumbly,' panted Mr Majeika, putting the clock down with a bump behind his stall. 'That's the sort of thing people want to buy, isn't it, Mr Potter. Old stuff that's been left lying about?'

'Why, certainly,' said Mr Potter. 'You've done very well to get hold of that, Majeika.' He peered at the clock again through his glasses. 'Hm, it looks a nice one,' he muttered to himself. 'Might bid for it myself if no one buys it. Looks just like my own – it would be fun to have a pair.' He was going to ask Mr Majeika what price had been put on the clock, but Mr Majeika had already gone again.

Five minutes later he was back, staggering under the weight of a huge leather-covered armchair. 'Well done again, Majeika,' Mr Potter remarked, as he bent over his vegetables. 'Just the sort of chair I like. In fact I've got one exactly like it.' But Mr Majeika, who had really got up steam now, had already disappeared.

By the time the Village Show opened at half past two, the Jumble Stall was entirely filled up to overflowing. A desk, two excellent dining chairs, some silver knives and forks, and some fine antique plates were among the choice items. 'Hm,' murmured Mr Potter as he strolled past the stall. 'Majeika has done well. Didn't think he had it in him. And funny how there must be people in the village with exactly the same taste in furniture and plates and things as I have. Why, everything on that jumble stall is exactly like something in my house.'

'Motley & Daughter', read the sign on the side of the furniture van. 'We Buy Junk, We Sell Antiques.'

The van was driven by a crafty-looking man with a red face (Motley). A shady-looking woman in a dirty flower-patterned dress (Daughter) sat by his side. They spent their weekends driving round the jumble sales, buying up items that people had under-priced and selling them for ten times the amount to city antique dealers.

They parked the van behind Much Barty village hall and slipped in just as Mr Potter was finishing his speech.

'Miss Painswick is here once again,' he was saying, 'to tantalize our tastebuds with her multi-farious jars of lemon curd, and though Mrs Hibbs can't be with us this year on Redcurrant Jellies, Miss Dursley has kindly stepped in – the same Miss Dursley who was so successful last year supplying stone gnomes for our gardens. And this year, for the first time, one of our, um, *prominent* pupils from St Barty's has been given his own little stall. Hamish Bigmore, ladies and gentlemen, will be selling Clothespeg Dollies.'

There was a round of applause, and Melanie stuffed her handkerchief into her mouth to stop herself laughing. At his stall, Hamish Bigmore stood glaring at everyone.

'He's not really going to sell those things, is he?' asked Thomas, pointing at the cute little dollies on Hamish's stall.

'Mummy thinks she's persuaded him to,' said Melanie. 'But I bet he runs off the moment the thing starts.'

'And finally,' said Mr Potter, 'a special thank you to Mr Majeika for taking the plunge and running the Jumble Stall. And just look what a magnificent collection of jumble he's assembled! Off you go, ladies and gentlemen. Spend, spend, spend!'

Several customers headed for the Jumble Stall but they were elbowed aside by Motley and Daughter, who had made a beeline for it when they saw all the antique furniture, silver and plates.

'Can I interest you in anything, sir?' asked Mr Majeika politely.

'Mebbe you can,' said Mr Motley.

'Good stuff 'ere, Dad,' said his daughter. 'And this bloke looks a right charlie, bet 'e'll let us 'ave it cheap.'

'Shurrup, Felicity,' muttered Mr Motley. 'Well, mate?' he asked Mr Majeika. 'How much is it?'

'How much is what?' asked Mr Majeika cheerfully. 'Everything has a different price, you know.'

'I know that, you ninny,' growled Mr Motley. He pointed at the grandfather clock. 'What d'you want for that, f'r instance?'

Mr Majeika thought for a moment. He had never really got the hang of Britland money. He rarely had to go shopping, as he lived in Walpurgian style, off wild plants and herbs from the hedgerow. He knew that there were pounds and pence. Pounds sounded rather a lot, and this man who was interested in the grandfather clock looked rather poor; probably he couldn't afford to pay in pounds. 'Let me think,' said Mr Majeika. 'How about four pence?'

'Mr Motley's jaw dropped. 'Come on, mate,' he said.

Obviously, thought Mr Majeika, the man couldn't afford as much as four pence. 'All right,' he said. 'To you, three pence.'

Mr Motley stared at him. 'You serious?' he asked. He leant over and whispered in his daughter's ear. 'Felicity, we got a right raving nutter 'ere. This could be our day.' He handed over ten pence. 'Three from ten is seven,' he said to Mr Majeika, as if talking to a child. 'What can you let me have with the change, mate?'

Mr Majeika thought for a moment. Seven pence must be a lot of money if you were poor. 'Well,' he said, 'I suppose for seven pence you could have everything.'

'Everything?' said Mr Motley in total disbelief.

'Stark raving loony,' muttered his daughter. 'Take the lot, Dad, and run.'

'That's all right,' said Mr Majeika, who had heard these last words. 'No need to run. I'll help you carry everything out.'

The Motleys were fast movers and in a few moments everything had gone except for a large wardrobe, which Mr Majeika had carried down with some difficulty from Mr Potter's bedroom. (Mr Potter's clothes were still in it.)

Just at this moment, Hamish Bigmore escaped at last from the clutches of Mrs Brace-Girdle. She was manning the stall next to Clothespeg Dollies herself, and she had managed to keep an iron grip on him. But a rush of customers turned up for her jam tarts and for a moment she let go. In an instant, Hamish had disappeared. Diving under the stalls, he looked this way and that for somewhere to hide until the Village Show was over. He knew that if Mrs Brace-Girdle caught even a glimpse of him, he'd be her prisoner again.

Then he saw the wardrobe.

'That's the lot, Dad,' said Miss Motley. 'Let's get out of 'ere quick before the nutter changes his mind.'

'Wait a mo, Felicity,' said Mr Motley. 'Don't forget that wardrobe. Nice piece of Hepplewhite-Chippendale, that is. Sell for two hundred quid, that will. Maybe three hundred. 'Ere, give us a hand. It ain't 'alf 'eavy.'

* * *

140

'Melanie,' said Thomas.

'Yes?'

'I think Hamish Bigmore was hiding in that wardrobe.'

'What wardrobe?'

'The one Mr Majeika has just sold.'

'Well, well, Majeika,' said Mr Potter cheerfully at the end of the afternoon, 'another vintage year. Couldn't have enjoyed myself more. I won again, you know. Biggest in the show.'

'Oh, well done, Mr Potter,' said Mr Majeika eagerly.

'And you, Majeika? Everything sold, I see?'

Mr Majeika nodded. 'Oh yes, Mr Potter. It was sold very quickly.'

'Got a good price for it, I hope, Majeika?'

Mr Majeika thought for a moment. 'I should say it was a pretty good price, Mr Potter.'

'Good, good,' said Mr Potter. 'And now, why don't we all go back to School Cottage for tea?'

'Felicity?' said Mr Motley, as the van bumped down the road out of Much Barty. 'Can you 'ear a funny noise back there?'

'What sort of noise, Dad?'

'A sort of banging and shouting?'

Felicity listened for a moment. 'Yeah, Dad,' she said. 'I can. Sounds like it's coming from that old wardrobe.'

'What d'you think it is, Felicity?'

Miss Motley thought for a moment. 'Mice,' she guessed.

'Too noisy for mice, Felicity.'

Miss Motley thought again. 'Well, then,' she said, 'maybe it's woodworm.'

'Yes, I'd love to have a cup of tea at School Cottage, Mr Potter,' said Mrs Brace-Girdle. 'But there's just one thing. I can't find Hamish Bigmore.'

'Ah, well,' said Mr Potter, 'I expect he'll turn up. Let's just enjoy his absence while we can, shall we?'

'I suppose so,' said Mrs Brace-Girdle. 'But we really ought to search for him. You know how easily that child can get up to trouble. By the way, Mr Majeika, how much money did you make on your stall?'

'Ten pence,' said Mr Majeika cheerily, holding out the money.

Mrs Brace-Girdle frowned. 'Ten pence?' she repeated. 'And how many pounds?'

'No pounds, Mrs Brace-Girdle,' Mr Majeika explained. 'Just ten pence.'

'Just *ten pence*? I don't believe it. All that stuff sold, and you – '

'Now, now, Bunty,' said Mr Potter soothingly. 'I expect there's a misunderstanding somewhere. We'll sort out all the money side when we've sat down with a nice cup of tea. It's been a long afternoon. Why, it must be almost six o'clock.' He pushed open the front door of School Cottage.

142

'That's odd,' he said. 'Whatever's happened to the grandfather clock?'

'You stupid, stupid, *stupid* little man!' Mrs Brace-Girdle was shouting at Mr Majeika. 'You ludicrously idiotic . . .'

'But I still don't understand, Mrs Brace-Girdle,' Mr Majeika was saying pathetically. 'I was only doing what Mr Potter told me to. He asked me to find a lot of old things and sell them, and that's just what I did.'

'I didn't mean *my* things, Majeika,' said Mr Potter faintly. He had collapsed in a heap on a kitchen chair – one of the few pieces of furniture left in School Cottage – and was scarcely able to speak.

'We ought to call the police,' said Mrs Brace-Girdle. 'We ought to have you arrested, Mr Majeika, for breaking and entering, for burglary. You could be locked up for years and years and years!'

'It wasn't his fault, Mummy,' pleaded Melanie.

'He didn't understand,' said Thomas.

'Don't be ridiculous,' snorted Mrs Brace-Girdle. 'Not his fault indeed! Whose fault was it, I'd like to know? Not Hamish Bigmore's, for certain. This is one crime that needn't be laid at the door of that particular individual.'

'Hamish Bigmore!' said Thomas. 'Cripes, I'd quite forgotten!'

'Forgotten what?' asked Mrs Brace-Girdle sternly.

'Forgotten Hamish Bigmore, Mummy,' said Melanie. 'You know that wardrobe of Mr Potter's that Mr Majeika sold? Well, Hamish Bigmore was inside it.'

Up at Much Barty Police Station, Sergeant Sevenoaks was taking down details.

'Speak more slowly, madam,' he said down the telephone to the highly harassed Mrs Brace-Girdle. 'I want a full description of everything that's missing.'

'I've told you already,' snapped Mrs Brace-Girdle into the phone. 'There's a wardrobe and a small boy in it.'

'A – ward – robe,' repeated Sergeant Sevenoaks slowly, as he wrote down the word in his notebook.

'He's medium height for his age, with black hair.'

'Me – dium height,' wrote down Sergeant Sevenoaks laboriously. 'Black hair. Funny sort of wardrobe. Now, what does the small boy look like?'

'Don't worry,' said Melanie to Mr Majeika. 'You can find him, can't you? And all the furniture?'

'Surely all you have to do,' said Thomas, 'is to flick your hair?'

'Just one flick, that will do, won't it?' said Melanie.

Mr Majeika slowly shook his head. 'It would

have done,' he said miserably. 'Certainly it would have done. But I can't.'

'Can't what?' asked Thomas.

'Can't flick it. I can't wiggle my hair at all today. I've just washed it, for the first time in sixty-two years, Thomas, and I can't do a thing with it.'

'Then, there's only one thing for it, Mr Majeika,' said Thomas. 'You've got to tell the Worshipful Wizard what's happened.'

'And be booted into everlasting Walpurgian Darkness for being so stupid, Thomas? No, no!'

'I'm sure he'll understand,' said Melanie.

'*Not in trouble again, are we, Majeika?*' said a voice in Mr Majeika's ear.

'It's him!' whispered Mr Majeika to the children. 'He must have been listening all along.' He cleared his throat nervously. 'Little spot of bother, I'm afraid, sir,' he said to the Worshipful Wizard. And, in a great fluster, he did his best to explain . . .

'*Now, let me get this straight, Majeika,*' said the Worshipful Wizard about ten minutes later. '*Are you really telling me that you've lost the entire contents of a cottage plus one small boy?*'

'Yes, sir,' said Mr Majeika miserably.

'*Well, well, you have exceeded yourself this time, Majeika. And I suppose this once I'll have to sanction the use of – Walpurgian methods.*'

'Magic, sir? Oh, thank you, sir, very kind of you, sir. But I'm afraid that's impossible.'

'*Impossible?*' said the Worshipful Wizard. '*Oh, come now, Majeika, you may be a Failed Wizard of the Third Class Removed, but it shouldn't be beyond your*' powers to think up some suitable piece of magic to help the present situation?'

'Oh, no, sir, not at all, sir,' said Mr Majeika. 'But you see – sixty-two years had gone by since the last time, and today – well, I don't know how to put this . . .'

'*Don't tell me, Majeika, I can guess. You washed your hair.*'

Mr Majeika sighed and nodded.

'*So where is Hamish Bigmore now, Majeika?*' asked the Worshipful Wizard.

'Well, sir, I don't know. I've absolutely no idea. None whatsoever. I was hoping that you might be able to help . . .'

'*Not me, Majeika,*' said the Worshipful Wizard. '*This is your problem. Do your best, Majeika.*'

'How's it going, Sarge?' Police Constable Bobby asked Sergeant Sevenoaks.

'Not bad, Constable, not bad. We've got Identikit pictures of this here wardrobe circulated to half the police forces in Europe.'

'But are you any nearer to solving the crime, Sarge?'

Sergeant Sevenoaks thought for a moment. 'No, Constable, I wouldn't exactly say that. Maybe this is going to be a case for – Scotland Yard.'

'Scotland Yard!' said Police Constable Bobby, thoroughly impressed. 'Are you going to telephone them, Sarge?'

'I am,' said Sergeant Sevenoaks importantly. 'I wonder what their number is, Constable? I expect

Directory Enquiries will know. Oh, and Constable, would you mind lending me ten pence for the phone?'

'*Do your best!*' repeated Mr Majeika bitterly. 'How can I do my best, when my tuft won't work?'

'I've got an idea,' said Melanie. 'The trike.'

'Yes, I was wondering about that,' said Thomas. 'Does it need magic from you to make it work, Mr Majeika, or has it got a will of its own?'

'It's certainly got a will of its own,' answered Mr Majeika. 'It can be thoroughly tiresome when it's in a bad mood.'

'Well, let's be as nice to it as we can,' said Melanie, 'and maybe it will help us find Hamish and the wardrobe and all Mr Potter's furniture.'

The trike was in a thoroughly bad mood at first, and it took Mr Majeika nearly half an hour to tame it and make it come to him when he called. And then when he had explained what he wanted it to do, it bucked about like an angry horse. It was only when Melanie had patted it on the saddle and said all kinds of nice things about what a lovely trike it was, that it quietened down and seemed ready to help them.

'Well, *Majeika?*' said the voice of the Worshipful Wizard. '*Any progress?*'

'Oh yes, sir,' panted Mr Majeika, who was speeding along a country road at a breakneck pace.

'Trike being very helpful, sir. Hamish in sight already.'

And indeed, a little in front of Mr Majeika, was the Motleys' furniture van, driving as fast as it could.

'I fink we're being followed, Felicity,' said Mr Motley, looking in the driving mirror. 'It's that nutter from the jumble stall.' He took a sharp right turn off the main road. The trike, realizing what had happened too late to correct itself, sped on straight ahead.

'Oh, bother!' said Mr Majeika. But a moment later he added, 'Oh, well done, trike!' For the tricycle had risen in the air, and was flying over the countryside, so that soon they were hovering right above the van.

'And another thing, trike,' said Mr Majeika, 'all this wind should dry my tuft properly.'

'Well done, Dad,' said Miss Motley, looking in the mirror. 'Reckon we've shaken him off good and proper.'

'No we ain't!' yelled her father. 'Look out!' Right in front of them, having appeared out of nowhere, stood Mr Majeika with his tricycle, in the middle of the road, holding up his hand like a policeman.

Mr Motley swerved to avoid him, crashed the van through a fence, and ground to a halt in the middle of a muddy field.

Miss Motley wound down a window. 'It's a fair cop, guv,' she said to Mr Majeika.

'So sorry to bother you,' said Mr Majeika, 'but

I'm afraid I'm going to have to give back the ten pence.'

The Motleys' van reappeared in Much Barty about half an hour later, having been towed backwards all the way by Mr Majeika – whose tuft was now working perfectly – and the trike. Grumpily, the Motleys unloaded the furniture and carried it all back into School Cottage. Even more grumpily, Hamish Bigmore helped them.

'Case closed, Sarge?' asked PC Bobby as he watched from the door of the police station.

'Afraid so, Constable,' said Sergeant Sevenoaks sadly. 'Pity you hadn't got that ten pence for the phone.'

'I don't think I'll do Jumbly again next year, Mr Potter,' said Mr Majeika as he helped the head-master to put the china and knives and forks away. 'It's not really in my line.'

'No,' said Mr Potter, 'I don't really think it is, Majeika.'

'I'd stick to something safe, Mr Majeika,' said Melanie.

'What sort of thing do you suggest?' asked Mr Majeika.

'Maybe a White Elephant stall?' said Thomas.

Mr Majeika brightened up. 'That sounds fun,' he said. 'But where on earth am I going to find white elephants?'

6

BLESS THE BRIDE

It was raining. Raining very hard. So hard that it seemed as if someone up there in the sky was crying buckets and buckets.

'Mr Majeika! Mr Majeika!' Despite the rain, Thomas and Melanie had run all the way to the windmill, sharing a mackintosh held over their heads, to see what Mr Majeika was up to on this wet afternoon.

But when they knocked on the door, there was no reply. 'Perhaps he can't hear us with the noise of all this wind and rain,' said Melanie.

'No,' said Thomas. 'It's not that. Look! He's hung his bat out upside down.' On the front door, hanging by its feet like a door knocker, was Mr Majeika's pet bat that he had been given for his birthday. 'When Walpurgians do that,' explained Thomas, 'it means *Do Not Disturb*.'

'Oh,' said Melanie. 'Well, I wonder what he's up to . . .?'

Mr Majeika was on the upper floor of the windmill. He had not heard the children knocking, or he would have come down, despite the Do Not Disturb sign. His mind was elsewhere; he was looking through his photograph album.

He turned the pages slowly. Ten pages were headed *Qualified Wizards of Walpurgis*. There, posing for the camera, were all his old friends – Wizard Spitt, Wizard Spells, Wizard Thymes and many more; all his old acquaintances from Sorcery School who, one by one, had passed their exams and been invested with all the powers of wizardry. Then there was a page, a single page, headed *Unqualified Wizards*. There was just one photo on this page: his own. He turned the page quickly and so came at last to what he was really looking for: *Witches*: Class of '07.

Yes, there they were, all the pretty young Witches with whom he had been at school back in 1807, the year in which – if he had passed his Sorcery Exams – he would have qualified as a Wizard. He could put a name to every face. There was Moody Garland, so-called because she got into dreadful moods and always wore a garland of deadly nightshade around her neck; when she was cheerful she was always singing songs about rainbows. There was Mad Donna, who wanted to be a pop star when she left school; Mr Majeika wondered what had happened to her? There was Wilhelmina Worlock – oh dear! Mr Majeika turned the page quickly. And there was – Myrtle Bindweed!

Myrtle Bindweed! The very sight of those fair features quickened his heart. The Witch of his dreams. Ah, the loving little notes they had passed to each other in the back row of old Stinks's Spells Class! Ah, how he had waited to carry her broomstick after school! Ah, how his heart had ached when she had forsaken him for Wizard Beano, who was always reading comics and didn't really care about girls at all. And so they had drifted apart, though Mr Majeika could still recall every feature of dear Myrtle – her long black talons, the way she knotted her hair with the plant after which she was named, the specially long teeth she put in to chew her school lunch. Ah, Myrtle, Myrtle, what could have become of her?

'Feeling homesick, Majeika?' said a voice in Mr Majeika's ear.

'Now and again, sir. And a little lonely, too. Lonely for a special person . . . Of course, it was a long time ago now, sir. She'd be two hundred and thirty by now, sir.'

'You are referring, I assume, to Miss Wilhelmina Worlock?'

'Her, sir? Most certainly not, sir! No, that particular female could never be described as the woman of one's dreams. More the woman of one's nightmares. No sir, my heart belongs to another . . .' And tenderly, Mr Majeika picked up the photograph album and kissed the picture of Myrtle Bindweed.

''Tis love, as somebody said, that makes Walpurgis go round,' remarked the Worshipful Wizard.

'Quite so, sir.'

'And there's a lot of it about, Majeika. A lot of it about.'

* * *

152

There was indeed. Love for flowering in – of all places – School Cottage.

It had been raining in Much Barty for days and days and days (you really *would* have thought someone was weeping up there in the sky), and Mr Potter had caught a bad cold. He was sitting in his armchair – the one that Mr Majeika had rescued from Motley and Daughter – and sneezing his heart out. But at least he wasn't lonely. Someone was looking after him, with all the care that an elderly unmarried lady can lavish on a bachelor headmaster. Someone had provided a mustard bath for his feet. Someone had wrapped a shawl around his shoulders. Someone was bringing him a clean hanky. Someone was bustling to and fro with thermometers and medicines and warm flannels and hot beef broth.

'You know,' said Mr Potter, sneezing again, 'you really shouldn't wait on me hand and foot like this, Nanny Jelley.'

'But I love waiting on you, Dudley,' said Flavia Jelley. 'It's all a woman could dream of.' Tenderly, she wiped a drip from the end of his nose.

Hamish Bigmore, who was still living at School Cottage, had behaved himself a bit better since the business of the Iron Lady, and though Nanny Jelley wasn't fierce any more, she knew now how to keep the wretched boy under control. So she had much more time to devote to Mr Potter.

'Oh, Dudley,' she sighed, looking into his bloodshot, watery eyes.

'Oh, Flavia,' crooned Mr Potter, and tenderly, they clasped hankies.

Down, down, came the rain. Would it never end? Up there in the sky, someone must be positively sobbing.

Someone was. Tears were gushing forth from Walpurgis by the gallon, and falling straight down on Much Barty. And those tears were originating in the Witches' Knitting Circle, where a big fat figure was howling her heart out, stopping only to fetch herself another huge black hanky.

'There, there, lovey,' said Witch Hazel, the Chief Knitter, handing round more balls of cobwebs to the other knitting witches. 'Cheer up, lovey. Knit two, drop three.'

'Cheer ups? Cheer ups?' spluttered the sobbing figure. 'How cans I cheer ups, Witch Hazel, when all the whiles I knows I is the only Witch here wot ain't got someone's Love Token Ring on her finger?'

'There, there, lovey,' soothed Witch Hazel. 'I'm sure some day your Wiz will come.'

'But I ain't got times for *some days*, Witch Hazel,' groaned Wilhelmina Worlock. 'I is a Witch in the prime of me womanhood, and times is running out.'

'Yes,' muttered Witch Hazel, looking at the shapeless mass of Wilhelmina, 'maybe it is.'

'And it's very hards,' sighed Wilhelmina, 'for a woman to be losing her looks – before she's even found a mans to blame for losing 'em!'

'Surely you were engaged to be married once, weren't you, Willy dear?'

Wilhelmina groaned again. 'Yerrs, I was. To a weasly worm of a Wizard wot threw me over like the skin off a Mice Pudding.'

'Really, lovey? Are you talking about poor Majeika? Knit ten, drop eleven.'

'Poor Majeika! I'll give him poor Majeika!' spluttered Willy Worlock. 'He threw me over, Witch Hazel, because he had the hots for ones Myrtle Bindweed, the dirty bat. Myrtle Bindweed, thats scrawny littles thing from the Lower Fourth! Wots gave him her glads eye on Walpurgis Night when I was in the Witches' Room powdering my warts.'

'But lovey . . . Knit twelve, drop fifty . . . If he really did propose to you once – ?'

'He did, Witch Hazel. He asked me to marry him, though he was deliriouses at the time with a dose of the mange.'

'And if it was written down in the Book of Promises?'

'Oh it was, I made sure of thats.'

'Then he's honour bound to marry you, eventually,' said Witch Hazel.

'But I ain't got time for *eventually*,' sighed Willy Worlock. 'I wants to be his Bride *nows*, Witch Hazel.'

'I can see that, lovey. But how are you going to get your talons on him? You know he can't stand you.'

Wilhelmina Worlock sighed deeply. 'Last time I went downs, Witch Hazel, he made a wish that he wouldn't see me again for a very long time. So what am I going to do about that, eh?' She thought for a moment, dabbing her eyes and sniffing. 'Of course,' she said after a while, 'if he didn't see *mees* . . . If he saw someone *elses* . . .?'

'What do you mean, lovey?'

Willy Worlock got to her feet with a sudden firmness of purpose. 'I've got it, Witch Hazel! I'm goings to visit him in disguise!'

'Disguised as what, deary?' asked Witch Hazel, surveying the enormous bulk of Wilhelmina. 'You'd look quite good as a rhinoceros.'

'No, no, don't you sees? I'm going to visit him disguised as Myrtle Bindweed.'

'So, sir,' Mr Majeika was saying, 'if you could possibly arrange a little female companionship? Just a little visit from a certain Witch . . .?'

'*Well, Majeika, I'll see what I can do. Is there a particular Witch you have in mind?*'

'There is indeed, sir. A young lady by the name of Myrtle Bindweed. You'll know her at once by her yellow hair, sir. And her yellow teeth. She's a real beauty, sir. You can't miss her. I think she usually hangs about in the Witches' Knitting Circle.'

'*I'll do my best, Majeika.*'

'Oh, thank you, sir!'

There are an awful lot of Wizards and Witches in Walpurgis, and the Worshipful Wizard did not know the names of more than half. So when he went to call on the Witches' Knitting Circle and met a big fat Witch coming out to meet him, who had bright yellow hair and said her name was Myrtle Bindweed, he had no reason to suppose that she was telling him a lie. And the blonde wig that Wilhelmina Worlock had acquired could certainly pass for her own hair, at least in the Walpurgian dusk with the light behind her.

The real Myrtle Bindweed, by the way, had left Walpurgis about a hundred years ago, to marry an Abominable Snowman, and had gone to live with him on the upper slopes of Everest.

'It's stopped raining at last,' said Melanie, and she and Thomas took off the mackintosh. 'The sky's quite clear now.'

'There's just one small black cloud,' said Thomas. 'It's moving very fast. In fact I wonder if it's a cloud at all . . . It looks awfully like a Walpurgian coming down to visit Mr Majeika.'

'Well, one thing's certain, it can't be Wilhelmina Worlock, not after the wish he made at the birthday party. That's a relief, isn't it?'

'I suppose so,' said Thomas. 'But there's something about the shape of that cloud that does remind me of her.'

The visitor from Walpurgis landed just outside the Barty Arms. Carrying her carpet bag, she marched through the front door of the pub, pausing only to check her wig in the hall mirror before she rang the bell on the desk.

'Why, hello, Miss Worlock,' said Harry the land-lord, emerging from the bar to answer the bell. 'Back with us again?'

The blonde-haired lady with the carpet bag shook her head, and answered in a broad American accent. 'Why, ma friend, you must be under some misapprehension. Y'are mistakin' me, I do surmise, for ma dear friend, the beauteous Miss Worlocks. And who cans blames yous, when we do in fact share the same similar set of stunning facial features? However, I is, in facts, Miss Myrtle Bindweed.'

'So sorry, I'm sure,' said Harry, pushing the visitors' book across to the lady. 'Staying long, are you, Miss Bindweed?'

'Just as long as it takes,' answered the visitor.

'Takes, Miss Bindweed?'

'Why, takes to be married – cutey-pie!' And Miss Myrtle Bindweed stretched out a talon and play-fully tweaked Harry's cheek.

'You mean,' gasped Harry, trying not to show his astonishment, 'someone in Much Barty is going to – *marry* you?'

'They certainly ares, honey-lamb. Only, they don't knows it yets!'

Thomas and Melanie ran to the windmill. 'Mr Majeika! Mr Majeika!' they called.

Mr Majeika came out of the front door and waved hello to them.

'Mr Majeika! There's someone come down from Walpurgis!'

'Goodness,' said Mr Majeika. 'Can it be *her* already?'

'Who, Mr Majeika?'

'Oh, never mind,' said Mr Majeika, embarrassed. 'Just . . . someone I was expecting.'

'She looked awfully like Wilhelmina Worlock when she was floating down from Walpurgis,' said Thomas. 'But she's checked in at the Barty Arms under the name of Myrtle Bindweed.'

'Oh!' cried Mr Majeika, looking up at the sky. 'Thank you, thank you, sir!' And before the children could say another word, he had rushed off at top speed to the Barty Arms.

Near the pub, he met Mr Potter, who was waiting outside a shop called Barty Brides, which sold wedding dresses.

'Ah, Majeika,' said Mr Potter. 'I have some glad tidings for you. My bachelor days are over. I have been swept off my feet, Majeika.'

Mr Majeika looked at Mr Potter's feet. 'You're still standing on them, Mr Potter.'

'I speak metaphorically, Majeika. I am betrothed – to the most bewitching woman in Much Barty!'

'Really, sir? Golly! And which Witch is that?'

'You are acquainted with the lady, Majeika. We all know her as – Nanny Jelley.'

At that moment, Miss Jelley emerged from Barty Brides laden with parcels. 'Coo-eee! Dud-leee!' she called to Mr Potter.

'My love!' called Mr Potter. Then he turned to

Mr Majeika. 'Tell me, Majeika, have you never contemplated matrimony yourself?'

Mr Majeika sighed. 'I would have, Mr Potter, but alas, I lost my true love many years ago. I have a little memento of her.' Hanging around Mr Majeika's neck was a small gilded locket.

'Charming, charming,' murmured Mr Potter. 'It contains a lock of her hair?'

Mr Majeika opened the locket. 'No, Mr Potter, just one of her front teeth.'

'Ah . . . Well, Majeika, maybe one day she'll come back to you.'

'Mr Potter,' said Mr Majeika, looking hopefully at the windows of the Barty Arms, 'I think she has!'

Miss Worlock was in her room at the Barty Arms adjusting her wig, when there came a tap at the door. She plucked up a fan from her dressing table and held it to her face before opening it.

'Miss Worlock?' asked Thomas, who was standing in the passage with Melanie.

'Pardonnez-moi,' said Wilhelmina Worlock. 'but I'm afraid you is mistaken, my little chickadee. I is the beauteous Miss Myrtle Bindweed. Now, if you'll excuse I – ' And she shut the door firmly in their faces.

Thomas and Melanie looked at each other. 'Well?' asked Melanie. 'Is she or isn't she?'

Mr Majeika had decided to go and gather a posy before calling at the Barty Arms. Thomas and

Melanie found him in the village street, carrying armfuls of wild mugwort that he had picked from the hedgerows. He was singing a sentimental Walpurgian ditty

We'll gather Mugwort in the murk again,
And walk together down a cobweb lane . . .

'Oh no!' said Thomas gloomily. 'Mugwort! Walpurgians only gather that when they're going courting.'

Mr Majeika pranced up to the Barty Arms, plucking petals off the mugwort and murmuring to himself: 'She loves me, she loves me not, she loves me, she loves me not . . .'

'Mr Majeika!' called Melanie. 'We want to warn you. We think that – '

But it was too late. A vast figure pushed its way out of the front door of the Barty Arms and elbowed the children aside.

Mr Majeika rushed forward. 'Myrtle!' he cried passionately. 'Is it really you?'

Miss Worlock blinked her false eyelashes at him. 'Pardonnez-moi,' she said, holding her fan carefully to her face, 'but do I knows you from somewheres?'

'Ah, Myrtle!' crooned Mr Majeika. 'Have you forgotten the Lower Depths Sedimentary School, where all the little Witches and Wizards begin their Walpurgian education? I used to carry your Spell Books after school.'

'Why, bristle ma broomsticks,' cooed Miss Worlock, 'if it isn't little . . . er . . . little?'

'Majeika, Myrtle. You haven't really forgotten, have you?'

'Yes, yes,' hissed Miss Worlock. 'I does sorta recalls you as one of ma many admirers.'

'Not just your admirer, Myrtle. Your partner at the 1806 Ugly Bug Ball. Oh, what a vision you were in your dress of Brussels Sprout Green, with an unforgettable pong of hemlock.'

'Yes,' drawled Miss Worlock, 'ah think ah do remember, come t' think of it. Well now, big boy, why don't ah come up and see yah some time?'

'Oh, Myrtle!' sighed Mr Majeika. *Would* you?' He pressed the bunch of mugwort into her arms.

'Say at bat-time this evenings, honey-bunch. I'll be right along.' And back into the Barty Arms she glided, pulling the heads off the mugwort and taking a good bite at the stalks.

Thomas and Melanie ran up to Mr Majeika. 'Mr Majeika! Listen! We don't know for certain, but we think that – '

But Mr Majeika was in a trance. 'Not now, children, not now.' And in a moment he was gone, heading for his windmill to look out his best clothes and dream of his tryst with Myrtle. *'We'll gather Mugwort,'* he sang happily to himself.

'I suppose we could be mistaken,' sighed Melanie. 'Perhaps all Witches from Walpurgis look like Wilhelmina Worlock.'

Thomas shook his head. 'Mr Majeika's Aunty Bubbles, who came down for his birthday party, didn't look like her at all. But we've got to be certain.'

Miss Worlock was having a little snooze in her room, to get up her strength for her romantic encounter with Mr Majeika. Thomas and Melanie could hear her snores echoing down the passage as they tiptoed up the stairs in the Barty Arms.

'She sounds as if nothing would wake her,' whispered Thomas, 'This is our chance.'

'All right, but don't forget,' warned Melanie, 'she is magical, Thomas.'

Very carefully and quietly, they opened the door. The great bulk of 'Myrtle Bindweed' was spread out on the bed, eyes closed, snoring like a steam engine. Her fan was over her face.

Thomas tiptoed across the floor, and very gingerly stretched out a hand to take hold of 'Myrtle's' hair. 'Yes!' he whispered. 'It's a wig.' Then he lifted the fan. 'Cripes! It *is* her.'

'Wilhelmina Worlock!' whispered Melanie. 'Of all the cheek, after Mr Majeika's wish . . .'

At the sound of her name, Miss Worlock had opened one eye. 'Gotchas!' she roared, making a grab for the children. Melanie screamed and Thomas tried to wriggle free, but they were held fast.

'Not thinkings of telling tales, are we, bratlings?' hissed Miss Worlock. ''Cos where I comes from, bratlings wot tells tales . . . grows tails!'

She pointed a finger at Thomas, and suddenly

163

he had a tail – a long curling tail like a lion's, ending in a tuft, which waved about behind him.

'Melanie!' called Thomas in dismay. 'Look!'

'And do yous want a tail too, little Miss?' hissed Miss Worlock.

'No!' answered Melanie anxiously.

'But gets one you wills if yous breathes one words of who I really is, to a certain Failed Wizard of the Third Class Removed. See? Does I makes myself clear, bratlings?'

'Yes, Miss Worlock,' said Thomas and Melanie.

'Goods,' said Miss Worlock, pointing a finger at Thomas so that his tail disappeared. 'So just you remembers that. Now out you gets!'

Mr Potter was . . . well, not beginning to have second thoughts about marrying Miss Jelley, but wondering quite what he had let himself in for.

Miss Jelley had been shopping every day for a week, buying her wedding dress, her veil, her shoes, her honeymoon clothes and a whole host of things Mr Potter had never even dreamt of. And he had to pay the bills. Now they were having a picnic supper on the banks of the River Barty and she was talking about spending even more of his money.

'For the Reception,' she was saying, 'I thought, Dudley, that you would order a stand-up buffet with cold salmon, and of course champagne.'

'Champagne, Nanny Jelley?' (He had got out of the habit of calling her Flavia.) 'B–but . . . I thought a glass of sherry and a fishpaste sandwich at the

164

Cherry Tree Tea Rooms would be quite enough, Nanny Jelley.'

Miss Jelley looked huffy. 'Well, it's my wedding, Dudley,' she said.

'Yes,' said Mr Potter miserably. 'Of course it is, my dear.'

A little further up the river, under the full moon, Mr Majeika was taking his lady-love out in a punt – the traditional place for Walpurgian courtship.

'Myrtle, my Mugwort?' he asked her, putting down the punt-pole.

'Yes, ma honey-bunch?' murmured 'Myrtle', carefully holding her fan in front of her face, as she did all the time. 'Myrtle, there's something I want to ask you. Something that, by Walpurgian tradition, can only be asked in a pea-green punt on a stagnant stream.'

'You means – you is proposing Matrimony, my little honey-lamb?'

'Wilt thou, Myrtle . . .?'

'Of course I wilts, Best Beloveds,' snapped Miss Worlock, forgetting her 'Myrtle' voice for the moment. 'You don't thinks I's gonna play hards to gets at my age, does you, Best Beloveds?'

'Oh no,' groaned Thomas, who, with Melanie, was watching from a bush on the bank. 'This is serious!'

'And for our honeymoon,' Miss Jelley was saying, while Mr Potter packed up the picnic hamper, 'I rather thought the South of France would do.'

'Abroad, Nanny Jelley?' asked Mr Potter anxiously. 'Won't that be rather . . . expensive? I had rather thought Mrs Laburnum's boarding-house at Barty Bay would suit us nicely, after the, um, expense of the wedding. You don't mind semolina pudding, do you?'

'Semolina pudding!' snorted Flavia Jelley. 'You think I'm going to eat semolina pudding on my honeymoon? This is my wedding, you know.'

'Yes,' said Mr Potter, in the depths of gloom. 'I know.'

On the way back to School Cottage Mr Potter saw two figures crossing a stile. 'Majeika!' he called. 'And if it isn't my old friend Miss Wilhelmina Worlock!'

'No, no,' cried Willy Worlock. 'Myrtle Bindweed. And you must bees the handsome and distinguished Mr Pottys. I've heard all abouts you from my dear friend Mr Majeika.'

'Not just your friend, Myrtle,' said Mr Majeika. 'Your fiancé.'

'Ah, that reminds me,' said Mr Potter, 'let me introduce *my* fiancée, Nanny – that is Flavia – Jelley.' The two brides-to-be shook hands. 'But Majeika, do I infer that you, too, are getting married?'

Mr Majeika nodded.

'At St Barty's and All Angels, Mr Majeika?' asked Flavia Jelley.

'No,' answered Mr Majeika. 'In Farmer Gurney's field.'

* * *

166

Up in Walpurgis, the Witches' Knitting Circle was hard at work with the needles when the telephone rang.

'What's that, lovey?' said Witch Hazel into the receiver. 'You've persuaded him? The wedding's finally on? At last? . . . Knit one, drop seventy . . . Oh, well done, Willy. And what's that? We're all invited?'

Farmer Gurney was moving his sheep into a field near Much Barty Aerodrome when a black balloon came down from the sky. A big box was dangling from it, and when it landed, the lid opened, and about two dozen Witches and Wizards, including the Worshipful Wizard himself, climbed out. They said 'Good afternoon' politely to Farmer Gurney and then set off up the road.

'Well, oi be danged,' said Farmer Gurney. 'Must have drunk too much zyder with moi lunch. Oi be zeeing things.'

At St Barty's and All Angels, the bells were ringing. Mr Potter was waiting at the church for his bride.

'Ah,' said the Vicar, rubbing his hands cheerfully, 'I do so love a wedding, don't you, Mr Potter? It's so awfully touching to see all that hope and optimism, before the . . . well, before the rot sets in.'

'Yes,' said Mr Potter glumly. 'Quite so.'

'I told you before,' snapped Hamish Bigmore, 'I'm not wearing a skirt.'

'But all Page Boys wear kilts at weddings, Hamish,' said Miss Jelley, who was all ready in her bride's dress.

'Don't care,' said Hamish Bigmore, undoing the kilt in which Miss Jelley had dressed him. 'It's sissy.' He chucked the kilt out of the window and ran full tilt out of the front door of School Cottage.

'Hamish!' called Miss Jelley. 'Come back! You'll spoil everything!'

Mrs Brace-Girdle put the finishing touches to Melanie's hair. Outside the bells were pealing. 'Come along,' she said briskly, 'off to the church. I'll follow as soon as I've put the finishing touches to the savoury flans for the reception.'

'All right, Mummy,' said Melanie. 'But Thomas and I have got to look in at another wedding on the way.'

'Another wedding?' asked Mrs Brace-Girdle suspiciously.

'Mr Majeika's.'

'Hm!' snorted Mrs Brace-Girdle. 'Well, I don't imagine *that* one will be at the church. Where is it, down at the Registry Office?'

'No, Mummy, it's in a haystack.'

'A *haystack*?'

The haystack had been specially built by the visitors from Walpurgis, under the instructions of Witch Hazel. 'That'll do nicely, loveys, knit two

168

purl two,' she announced, surveying the results. (She had left her knitting needles behind, but force of habit made her drop into knitting talk.)

At the Barty Arms, the brewer's horses and cart were all ready to transport 'Myrtle Bindweed' to Farmer Gurney's field. The front door of the pub opened, and there she was, in her wedding dress.

What a sight! The dress had been specially made of the smelliest pondweed, decorated with the skeletons of bats, and Miss Worlock's warts, carefully polished for the occasion, were gleaming in the sunlight.

She mounted the cart; a crack of the whip; and away she went.

Flavia Jelley was travelling to church by horse and cart too, but a very different sort of horse and cart – a smart little landau, pulled by a neat little pony, and driven by Miss Lammastide.

The church was only just around the corner from School Cottage, but Miss Jelley had decided to travel in style. Miss Lammastide was going to drive her out of Much Barty by one road, up and down the lanes, so that the local farmers and their families could come out to admire her, and then back into Much Barty and up to the church by another road.

The wedding was due to take place at twelve o'clock. At a quarter to twelve, they set off.

Hamish Bigmore knew about this plan. He had intended merely to wander the lanes around Much

169

Barty, knocking the heads off people's roses as he passed their cottage gardens, and if possible stealing some chocolates from somewhere or other. But when he came to a signpost, he had an idea.

The signpost had three arms. One said: 'To Much Barty.' Another said 'To the Aerodrome.' A third one said: 'To Barty Bottom. No Through Road.'

Hamish Bigmore took a look at the signpost for a few minutes. Then he turned it around, so that the signs were pointing in quite different directions.

A few moments later, the landau, driven by Miss Lammastide, and with Flavia Jelley in her wedding dress seated next to her, came trotting up the lane from the village. Miss Lammastide drew in the reins, the pony stopped, and she peered at the signpost.

'Now, Flavia,' she said, 'we need to take the Aerodrome road next.' She jerked the reins and the pony set off again.

Flavia Jelley peered around her. 'Are you sure this is the right road, Elsie?'

'Oh, certainly,' said Miss Lammastide. 'It's the way the signpost pointed.'

Behind the hedge, Hamish Bigmore grinned.

'Here she comes,' muttered Thomas to Melanie. They were hiding behind the haystack and watching, as Miss Worlock with a wedding veil hiding her face, descended from the brewer's cart.

170

'I wish she'd taken a wrong turning and got lost,' said Melanie. 'Still, I must say, she looks a picture.'

'Yes, but *what* a picture, Melanie.'

'But this isn't the Aerodrome, Elsie.'

'Are you sure, Flavia?'

'How could it possibly be an Aerodrome, Elsie? It's full of cows.'

The clock struck twelve. 'She's late,' said the Vicar.

'Yes,' said Mr Potter hopefully. 'She is.'

'Myrtle Bindweed' had gone inside the haystack, and Thomas and Melanie could hear the ceremony beginning.

'Nearly beloved brethren,' intoned the Worshipful Wizard, 'we are gathered here today to join this lovely Witch to this lucky Wizard, in matrimonial deadlock . . .'

'Oh, Myrtle!' whispered Mr Majeika, looking sideways at his bride, hidden behind her veil.

'Oh, Best Beloveds!' hissed Willy Worlock.

'Oh, cripes!' muttered Thomas, peering in through a chink in the hay. 'Melanie, isn't there anything we can do to tell him that he's really marrying *her*?'

'You remember what she said, Thomas. One word. She said if we open our mouths just once . . .'

'But if we didn't actually *speak*? If we somehow

let him know *without* opening our mouths . . .?
Quick, Melanie, I've got a plan!'

'But Thomas, why did we come to the windmill?
Oughtn't we to be at the haystack, if we're going
to stop the wedding?'

'Don't you see, Melanie? We've got to find some
way of *showing* him it isn't Myrtle Bindweed . . . A
photo or something . . . Look, here's his photo
album, maybe that will do the trick. No, wait –
here's something else. A locket, with "Myrtle Bindweed" and a heart engraved on it. I've seen him
wearing this around his neck. Let's look inside –
oh, yes! Yes! This'll do the trick!'

'It isn't fair!' sobbed Flavia Jelley. 'This road ought
to have led us into Much Barty, and here we are at
the Aerodrome!'

'Well, dear, I only followed the signpost.'

'No sign of her at all,' said the Vicar. 'I rather
think . . .'

'So do I,' said Mr Potter, trying not to look
pleased.

'Repeat after me,' intoned the Worshipful Wizard.
'I, Majeika . . .'
  'I, Majeika.'
  'Of the Windmill, Much Barty.'
  'Of the Windmill, Much Barty.'
  'Failed Wizard of the Third Class Removed.'
  'Failed Wizard of the Third Class Removed.'

'Do take thee, Myrtle.'

'Do take thee – whoops!' Mr Majeika put his hand to his neck. Something was tickling the back of it.

It was his locket, dangling from its chain. He looked up. Thomas had made a hole in the top of the haystack, and he and Melanie were looking in.

'Go away!' hissed Mr Majeika.

Thomas was pointing wildly at the locket.

'What do you want?' whispered Mr Majeika. Everyone was staring; the ceremony had come to a halt.

Thomas didn't speak. He kept on pointing at the locket. Mr Majeika opened it. There was nothing different about it. Myrtle's tooth was inside. He shut it again. Then a thought struck him. *Myrtle's tooth*.

Myrtle had given him that tooth when it fell out, after she had bitten a piece of bone in a batswing pie at the Ugly Bug Ball.

He peered at his bride, but he couldn't see her face because of the veil. He flicked his tuft, and by magic the veil lifted. Now he could see her smiling mouth. *And none of her teeth were missing.*

'Is it all over yets, your Worshipfulness?' the bride asked the Worshipful Wizard.

'It certainly is, Miss Wilhelmina Worlock!' said Mr Majeika.

'Oh lawks,' muttered Witch Hazel. 'He's found her out. Knit twelve, drop two hundred. She'd have done better to disguise herself as a hippo after all.'

* * *

'Why, yous littles . . .!' yelled Willy Worlock, bursting out of the haystack and making a grab for Thomas and Melanie as they lay on top of it.

'But we didn't say a word, Miss Worlock!' they told her. 'Not a word.'

'Of course,' remarked the Worshipful Wizard, 'as it is written in the Book of Promises, you will have to marry her one day, Majeika.'

'But not today, thank you, Your Worshipfulness.' He turned to the children. 'Thomas, Melanie, how can I ever thank you?'

'Don't worry, Mr Majeika,' said Melanie.

'We've still got wedding number two to go,' said Thomas.

'Wedding number two?'

'Mr Potter's. Come on, Mr Majeika, since your own's been called off, you'd better come to that one.'

'No, Majeika, I'm afraid we had to call it off. The lady in the case seems to have disappeared.'

'Really, Mr Potter? Well, I should think *my* lady will have disappeared by now. When I last saw her, she was packing up to go – and in an awfully bad temper.'

'Is that so, Majeika? Your own matrimonial proceedings became equally hitched? Well, well, Majeika. Can I give you a lift home on my motor bike?'

'Thank you, Mr Potter, how kind of you.'

Miss Jelley, covered in mud, was struggling back into the village on foot, having exchanged hard words with Miss Lammastide. A motor bike roared past, with Mr Majeika sitting in the sidecar. On the saddle, looking extremely pleased with himself, was Mr Potter.

'Dudley!' cried Flavia Jelley, 'come back! Oh, aren't men brutes!'

As she rose to Walpurgis, holding the string of her black balloon, Wilhelmina Worlock sobbed gently to herself, so that down below in Much Barty it began to rain again.

'Yous brutes!' she moaned. 'Yous brutes, Majeikas, yous brutes!'